FRISK

Dennis Cooper

A complete catalogue record for this book can be
obtained from the British Library on request.

The right of Dennis Cooper to be identified as the
author of this work has been asserted by him
in accordance with the Copyright, Designs and Patents
Act 1988

First published in 1991 by Grove Weidenfeld, New York

This edition first published in 1992 by Serpent's Tail,
4 Blackstock Mews, London N4

I'm very grateful to Walt Bode, Amy Gerstler, Richard Haasen,
Richard Hawkins, Hudson, Ira Silverberg, and Ken Siman.

"Paw Paw Negro Blowtorch" by Brian Eno, copyright © 1973
by E.G. Music Ltd. Used by permission of EG Music, Inc.
All rights reserved.

Printed by Mackays of Chatham, plc

10 9 8 7 6 5 4 3 2

for Mark Ewert

Contents

Put all the images in language in a place of safety and make use of them, for they are in the desert, and it's in the desert we must go and look for them.

—JEAN GENET

FRISK

He lies naked on a bed with his wrists bound, legs splayed, ankles secured to the corners. Striped sheet, tangled blanket. In the first shot his long, straight black hair's fallen over his face, covering everything but a greasy chin, which juts through the strands. He seems thirteen, fourteen. The genitals look like a weirdly shaped stone. His necktie is made out of a long piece of rope.

Two. Another medium shot. His hair curves sharply down either temple, sweeps back, and hooks over his ears like raised theater curtains. Longish face, pert nose. Dark eyes, glazed. Big mouth, too open. Otherwise he hasn't changed, I don't think. Same spindly legs, big feet tilting away from each other. Same crude necktie, bracelets, anklets.

Third shot's a close-up. His face, neck, tie, shoulders, arm-pits. His tongue's crumpled up in his mouth like a melted candle. His eyes could be parts of a doll. Each reflects the front

3

of a camera. His necktie's tied too tight; the rope is the kind that hoists anchors. If his eyes weren't such clouds, he'd appear to find something or someone hilarious.

Four's a medium shot. He's facedown, wrists and ankles undone. His arms are bent into neat, mirror L's. His ass sports a squarish blotch, resembling ones that hide hard-core sexual acts, but more sloppily drawn. His back, hips, and legs are pale and forgettable by contrast. His haircut's a shambles. His shoulders are dotted with zits.

Five. Close-up. The blotch is actually the mouth of a shallow cave, like the sort ocean waves carve in cliffs. The uneven frame of ass skin is impeccably smooth. The inside of the cave is gray, chopped-up, mushy. At its center's a pit, or a small tunnel entrance, too out-of-focus to actually explore with one's eyes, but too mysterious not to want to try.

WILD

1974

"Wild." Henry *knew* it. His feelings, thoughts, etc., were the work of people around him. Men particularly. The first made a weirdly detached person out of his body and mind when he was thirteen or something. The next man corrected his predecessor's mistakes. The next changed other stuff. The last few had only tinkered because Henry was perfect, aside from some bad habits.

He raised his glass, sipped, and tried to think about one particular "ex."

He threw the empty glass into the cold black fireplace.

The other young guy in the room seemed unbelievably stoned, drunk . . . something. He sat all the way across an ugly Indian rug, staring out or at a set of sliding glass doors. It sounded like it was raining. Henry couldn't see anything out there, even the rain.

"I'm so cold I'm a fucking ice sculpture, right?" Henry

asked loudly. The guy had said so, Henry was virtually sure. Still, it was hours ago, if ever. They'd squealed at the time, but the sentence was bullshit. It made Henry sound arrogant, which he probably wasn't.

The guy just stared off at the rain, glass, hallucination, daydream, whatever.

"I'm splitting," Henry said, stood.

The guy swiveled his head. *Crack*. "Don't . . . ouch." His head must have swiveled too quickly or something, because it started trembling like what's-her-name's . . . Katharine Hepburn's. He had to grab it with both hands to get it to stop.

This part's a blur.

"You know, it's wild," Henry said. He was fondling his way down a hall behind what's-his-name. ". . . but I don't even remember where we met tonight. I keep thinking 'party.' That's about it. Are you as totaled as I am?"

"Probably." The guy glared over his shoulder. He still looked cute enough to justify what was starting to happen, whatever that was. "Keep your hands down," he added. "I mean if you need to keep your balance, use the walls, not my father's African art collection."

"I am." Henry focused on the door at the end of the hall. He supposed they were aimed there, because it was open. No matter how low he reached on the walls he kept touching the limbs of wooden statues, so he gave up and clutched at the guy's untucked shirt.

"Don't fucking rip it."

"I'm *not*."

Henry flopped on the bed. It bounced around and squeaked for five, six seconds. The guy stripped. He had tiny red genitals, spider-webby blond pubic hair. Not that Henry cared about defects like that. He himself was a big waste of time from the neck down at this point, thanks to uncountable drugs.

"Get that stuff off," the guy mumbled.

"Oh, am I still dressed?" Henry toyed with a shirt button, twirling this way, that. Within a second or two he was spaced out. "Mm." He felt something sharp, fingernails, a hand, the guy's. It was yanking his underwear down. The pair got snagged around his feet. The guy left them dangling there. Henry's feet were huge. He raised up, peered down his chest. But blurry. "So, uh, I don't really know . . . what you, like . . . expect . . . to, like, get out of that." He pointed at his cock and said "that" again, sort of ironically.

"We'll . . . see . . ." The guy's face made a rocky landing on Henry's crotch.

"Oh, okay, go ahead." Henry let his head drop.

The guy started painting the cock with his tongue. The room felt cozy. Or the pills Henry took that afternoon left him cozy, and the room was just there, a movie set. He shut his eyes, tried to restart a favorite porn daydream. "Shi-i-i-it." His history had been reduced to a simplistic blur, like the trails in the air left by people on fire.

Blur.

"You know what?" Henry whispered, digging his hand into the guy's Afro. "I was thinking about this a minute ago in the other room. How last weekend I slept with two bearded guys. One of them fucked me while the other guy blew me, I guess. They kept calling me 'that.' One would ask, 'What does that taste like?' and 'What's the temperature inside that?' and the other would say, 'Really great,' or whatever. It made me feel weird. It made me realize I'm important to certain people. I don't have to do anything. Being pretty or young or whatever's enough. Sometimes . . . I wish I could just sort of temporarily die. Guys could move me around, whatever. I wouldn't have a first name, just a surface. Like pillows. They don't have individual names. They don't mean anything, but people sleep with them. I think I'd feel a lot happier, though I despise that word, 'happy.' It's such a lie. When your parents— Hey, wait!" He blinked a couple of times. The ceiling was totally in focus. "God, I'm sober." He propped himself up on his elbows. "What about you?"

The guy had quit blowing Henry earlier in the speech. His chin sat an inch deep in Henry's thigh. Henry's cock drooped down the other thigh, soft, brown, and extremely wet. "So," he mumbled, "does your not talking right now mean you agree with me, or that you're sleepy or something?"

"I think I'm sleepy," the guy said, staring. His face seemed the opposite of sleepy.

"Not me. But I'm infamous for my energy."

"So, you heading back to the party?" The guy's eyes actually pointed at Henry. They were pale blue. Like all eyes Henry had ever seen, but especially blue ones, they were sort of disappointing, apart from the color.

"I guess, yeah. You want to come?"

"Not really." The guy rolled onto his side, squashed the right half of his face with a fist. There was a Rorschach blot of sweat on the sheet where his crotch had been pressing. Henry looked down at it, thought he saw a satanic silhouette.

"Okay, uh . . ." Henry stood up, walked quickly around the room, bent over, collecting his clothes. "So, did you enjoy that?" He was missing a sock. "I mean was I . . . okay?" He checked behind the desk chair once more. "I know that's a weird question."

"I can't tell yet." The guy's voice was distorted because of the fist, so Henry couldn't quite get what the "yet" meant.

"Mm." Henry made a face that the guy could interpret a hundred ways, or not at all. By that point Henry was four-fifths dressed. He sat on a chair across the room, tying his shoes. "Well, answer this," he said. "I always ask this question after I sleep with somebody, so don't get alarmed. If you could change one thing about the way I was acting a minute ago, what would that be?" He quit tying, grinned. "I guess that's dumb."

"You talk too much," the guy said.

"Yeah, I know." Henry winced. "Thanks. I'm working on that one." He made a fist and slugged his thigh.

"And you don't consider what you say before you say it. Or you don't sound like you do." The guy slid off the bed, stood. He strolled around the room, stabbing a hand at his own crumpled clothes, which were larger and blacker than Henry's. "I'll show you the way out. Because I was really interested in you at first." He knelt down and peered under the bed. "But when you tried to tell me about . . . well, whatever you were saying when I started to get into you." He reached into the dark, pulled out an argyle sock, shook some dust off. "I can't be the only guy who's turned off by that kind of shit."

Henry cringed, nodded. The pills were wearing off to a slight degree. "No, no, no, you're right." He slugged his thigh again.

"Anyway . . ." The guy held out the sock to Henry. "Get *up*."

They inched down the hall. This time it wasn't particularly treacherous. Henry picked out the floor, statues, their pedestals, the guy's back, etc. So he didn't need anyone or anything, though he wobbled around a lot.

Julian nodded. "I completely agree. It's . . . just . . ." He leaned closer to Jennifer's ear, got a faint whiff of vomit. "Am I insane or is that guy—long black hair, faded work shirt, by the hors d'oeuvres table—staring at me?" Jennifer squinted. "Actually," she said, "I've been assuming it was me, but I think you're right." She asked some other drag queens in their vicinity to move, pointed his way "accusingly." When he noticed, she flipped him off. "Me?" he mouthed, looking around. "Yeah, *you*, asshole!"

Henry weaved through the room, sideswiping every fifth person en route. Their drinks sloshed around. One brunet threw a lit cigarette at his back, missed. Julian grabbed Jennifer's right biceps and squeezed. "Fucked up," he said with a grin, "but incredibly appealing, right?" Nod. By then Henry was near enough that they could pretty much tell which of them he'd been staring at. Julian flashed a little teeth in the corner of his sneer. "Leave," he mumbled. "You mind?" Her arm slid through his fingertips.

"Hi." Henry came to a kind of halt. His head turned violently to the right, left. Nice neck. "Where'd she go?" He had an out-of-town accent. "Who?" Julian asked. Henry winced. "Very funny. I mean that girl who was right . . . Oh, it doesn't matter. Hi." Julian decided the face was too horsey. When it was saggier that'd be trouble, in terms of attracting guys. At the moment it made him seem rural or heterosexual.

"You from the South?" Julian asked. Henry rolled his eyes. They looked sketchy and smudged. "No, that's totally weird," he said. "Nothing against you. People always say that, but it's not true. They only say it when I'm stoned, which I am, obviously. No, I'm from here . . . Oops." He slapped a hand over his mouth, opened his eyes so wide Julian had to think about the fact that they were balls. The balls sort of pleaded with Julian. "What?" he responded, not totally interested.

Henry said something, dismembered bits of which filtered through his fingers. "I decided," or maybe it was "I determined" (unintelligible) . . . "talk too much." He wasn't as cute without his chin and mouth. "Really?" Julian eased his ass down on the windowsill. He started scanning the room for a less wiped-out type. Someone he vaguely liked walked in, hugged someone he'd fucked twice. "You're saying you talk too much?" he muttered, studying the hug. Henry nodded.

Julian was wondering about the subtext of that particular hug when he remembered Henry. "Oh, I'm thinking about them," Julian said, nodding, "over there. Follow my nod."

Henry appeared to, then mumbled something about "near the door." "Exactly," Julian said, smiling. "Hey, want to try an experiment?" Henry shrugged. "Good. Hug me like you've known me forever but haven't seen me in years." Julian extended his arms, smirked. Henry blushed, took a baby step forward.

"Gotcha, as they say." Julian dragged Henry close. Henry opened his fingers a crack and pushed his big lips through. "Ouch. What do you mean?" "I mean," Julian said, peeling away Henry's hand, "now that we're old friends I can ask you for anything and you'll do it because we love each other." Henry wrenched back his head an inch or two, peered warily at Julian's mouth. "Is that a joke?" he asked. Henry looked sort of interesting cross-eyed. "Is what a joke?" "Is it a joke," Henry whispered, "that we love each other?"

"Christ," Julian groaned. "Are you one of those guys who think love's . . . whatever, sacred?" Henry shook his head. "Good, because as far as I'm concerned, love's what you feel for someone you don't know very well, if at all. Maybe I was 'in love' with your body when you were way over there studying Jennifer and me. Now I'm just, uh . . . hungry, you could call it. You being my . . . meal, or . . . what's the matter *now*?" Henry's face looked too attentive or something. "Yeah, yeah, I know!" he said loudly.

Heads turned. Julian let loose of Henry's ass. "No, don't let go! That's the point!" Henry picked up Julian's hands, hooked them over his hipbones. "Or wherever you had them. No, see, I've been figuring all this stuff out, and I agree! I'm like a thing, or like . . . a meal, or . . . whatever!" Everyone at the party was watching now, however furtively. Julian shielded his eyes, started chewing his bottom lip, mind whirling. The guy was wearing pink deck shoes. Cute. "Er, uh, let's go outside, okay?" Julian clutched Henry's hand. They zigzagged through their audience.

They pushed through a door clogged with drunken parents. The house had been built on a hillside. There were some steps carved in it that led up to a tilted vegetable garden. Julian dropped down on the third and fourth steps. Henry remained at their foot, smiling back at the house. Its windows were steamed. In the dirt below one was a puddle of purplish vomit, shaped exactly like Texas. "Now, what were we saying?" Julian yawned. Henry had started to teeter around pretty weirdly. "Oh . . . I forget. I, uh, feel . . . I guess, dizzy." He hiccupped, sat.

Julian reached out his hand, debated for a second or two, then let it penetrate Henry's long, slightly tangled black hair around the area of the nape. It was like a little cave under there. That gave Julian chills for some reason. He bunched his fingers and snaked them slowly along the narrow, curving tunnel, trying not to skim against the wall of hair on one side, or Henry's neck on the other. He managed to get about an inch and a half before Henry's left shoulder twitched, fucking everything up.

Julian traced the jagged part in Henry's hair with one fingertip. Back, forth, back, forth . . . Henry rested his chin in his hands, blew some air through his lips. "You want to come over to my place and sleep off whatever you're on?" Julian asked. The head swiveled a little. "I've already slept with somebody tonight." "Well, then, give me your number at least." Henry's forehead scrunched up. "Three . . . eight, five . . . four, four—" "Wait." Julian yanked out a pen, pressed its nub to the back of his hand. "Again."

"So he said it again. You know, three-eight-five—whatever, and I wrote it on the back of my hand. You can still see it. Then we had a long, slow kiss with lots of tonguing and stuff, and I left." Julian glanced at his wristwatch. "Left? Left?!"

I said, my voice tinny and sharp at the other end of the line. Julian held the receiver away from his ear. "Yeah, I had to see a client at two, unfortunately for everyone involved. Ugh." I started to say something. "Gotta go," Julian said. "See you in . . . about an hour?"

He traipsed into his bedroom, undressed, and stood in front of the full-length mirror. Over the past year or two he'd figured out how to look at himself with complete objectivity, at least in the nude. He squinted. His reflection fogged up, disconnected from him. Now he was a john—older, uglier, hornier. Was that cute kid in the mirror worth $100, $150? The cute kid smiled at Julian hopefully. *Scratch, scratch, scratch.* "What the . . . ?" Julian peered over the cute kid's right shoulder, refocusing his eyes.

His brother, Kevin, was out in the hall, slumped on the door frame, watching. One hand pawed his knee with a spidery motion. "So," Julian said, "what do you think of your bro, Kev?" Kevin blinked. "You *do* realize you can barge right on in," Julian added. Kevin's mouth tilted a bit, but his eyes remained fixed on Julian's ass, or on that general vicinity. "Hey, are you stoned or something?" Kevin shook his head, stepped in, turned stiffly, and clicked the door shut.

"What, is Mom on the rampage?" Julian said the word "Mom" in italics. It was one of the two or three words that always woke Kevin up when he spaced out like this. The kid's shoulders contracted an inch. "Sort of, yeah." "Well, sit." Kevin eased himself down on the edge of the bed, squeezed his knees tightly together, and jammed his fists in between them. "But can we not talk about it, Julian? Can we talk about something . . . I don't know?" He looked to his left. "About them?"

Kevin was looking painfully at the cover of the latest Black Sabbath LP. As usual, misery focused the kid in some way. Julian wanted to hug Kevin, or he didn't want to exactly, it just seemed appropriate. Still, he was naked, so that made it inappropriate for reasons too complicated to think about. "What about them?" Julian leaned back on the icy mirror. "Is it good?" Kevin asked. "Yeah, you want to borrow it?" The mirror felt great. "Sure." Kevin smiled weirdly.

"Do you want to do your big brother a favor?" Kevin's smile got less weird. Nod. "Well, first of all, do you ever think about sex?" Kevin brightened. "*Think* about it, yeah." His left leg started to tremble very slightly. "Okay, could you put yourself in a mental state where you could tell me if I was sexy or not? Like if you were a girl or a fag or whatever?" "Shit, Julian." Kevin clutched his stomach with both hands, tongue out, panting. His eyes looked hypnotized, transplanted . . . something.

Julian: "What?" Kevin drew in his tongue. "I don't know . . . ouch!" Julian watched him contort and groan, perplexed. Maybe the question was too complicated. It wasn't like sex was off limits. There were pairs of little Jockey shorts caked with dried come stashed in crannies all over the kid's bedroom. Julian had accidentally found them when he was scouring the house for drugs once. He'd even stolen a few pairs and given them out to friends as Christmas presents.

"I'm not saying you're gay, Kev. I'm not imposing that on you. Or if I am, which maybe I am, forget I asked. Really." That didn't help. The kid was bouncing all over the place, squawking, swallowing, grabbing at things. Jesus Christ, Julian thought. He folded his arms and walked up to the bed. "Lie down, Kev. Relax." "Oh, okay." Kevin fell backward, bounced a couple of times, then rolled over cautiously onto his stomach. He started crawling toward Julian's pillow.

Julian stood over Kevin and waited for something about him to change for the better. Kevin's back inflated, deflated more normally. He shut up. The insignia on his T-shirt quit resembling a saddle. Phew, Julian thought. He started fetching his clothes from the floor around the bed. Then he tiptoed back to the mirror and slipped them on, piece by piece. "Kev, you okay?" he asked between socks. The head in the pillow stirred. "We can talk about this later?" More motion.

A half hour later Julian perched on the edge of a chair in my parents' library. They'd gone out to dinner. The shelves were crammed with Reader's Digest Condensed shit. I turned the dial of a clock radio, making a rock opera from severed parts of announcements and ads and hit songs. That sounded eerie for a while, but . . . "Enough!" Julian yelled. I stopped at a violent guitar riff. "Dennis, I have to tell you about this thing with Kevin!" I turned down the volume a token amount. "Oh, gee, thanks a lot!

"Anyway, what happened was, he freaked out like he always does," Julian yelled. "But maybe this time it was worse. Hard to tell. It happened in my room, so, obviously, it would have seemed worse. Anyway, he was lying on my bed afterward trying to calm down, and I was standing there looking at him, not knowing what to do and everything, and I felt mesmerized by his ass. You could see it through his pants, because of the way he was lying, I guess. So—"

"Perv!" I switched off the radio. Julian smirked. "Maybe, but not for the obvious reason. Anyway, thanks. It was just . . . the thing was so perfect. It was like a . . . textbook ass. You know, a little boxy with rounded off corners and dents in the sides. Only Kevin's was so small that I couldn't have any kind of normal reaction to it at all. It was more like a toy than an ass, although that's not right exactly. I mean, it was my brother's ass, sure, but formally it was the ultimate ass, you know?"

I nodded and shrugged simultaneously. "I think," Julian continued, "it was the thing's scale. I don't know what it made me understand . . . that the body isn't inherently sexy? Partly, for sure. Or how Kevin's totally fucked up inside, but his body's so perfect outside, and what does that combination mean? I mean it's just . . . oh, fuck, I don't know." He shut his eyes, baffled. "Well, I think he's a doll," said my voice. "Who, Kev?" Julian started massaging his eyelids. That helped.

"It could be the mescaline, though," I added. Julian was studying the backs of his eyelids. When he turned away from the lamp, he saw reddish dark. Facing the lamp, teensy bits of graffiti appeared, flew about, shifting directions abruptly like UFOs. "Me too, I guess." He opened his eyes. I was rocking my chair, knuckles purplish-white barnacles on the armrests. *Creak, creak, creak, creak.* "Hey, I think I'm going to call this number on the back of my hand," he said, ". . . if I can still read it."

Creak, creak, creak. Julian held his hand under the lampshade and squinted. The last digit was either a 1 or a 7. He made a lunge at the phone and started punching in numbers. *Creak, creak, creak, creak.* "Are you sure this guy's cute?" I said nervously, almost hissing. "Because if he's not . . ." "Yeah, yeah, ssh." It was ringing. *Creak, creak . . .* Julian waved his hand at me frantically. "Ssh!" *Click.* "Hi." "Is Henry there?" "Speaking."

Henry's clothes looked too baggy, at least in the mirror. Still, they were close to the stuff he'd been wearing the night Julian liked him supposedly. He took three steps backward, switched the phone to his left ear, squinted.

"Okay, great," he mumbled. "It'll be nice to—" *Click.* ". . . to . . ." He hung up the phone. ". . . to see you again," he sighed, spacing out on his reflection.

Blur.

"Anyway . . ." He walked up to the mirror and unsnapped his jeans, which were so loose they plummeted to his shoes. He lifted the front of his T-shirt and fluffed out his black pubic hair, untangling a few little knots with his nails. "Fine." He held up his cock by the head, let it drop. *Thwap.* Again.

Thwap. "Hmm." He turned his pimply back on himself and bent way over, putting his ass in the best possible light. "Slurp," he joked aloud. Actually it might look okay, he thought, if the crack wasn't hairy. He spread the cheeks, eyed his "smelly mohawk," as one "ex" had described it.

Henry leaned there, daydreaming about that particular "ex." First the memory was general, him lounging around stoned in what's-his-name's mansion for weeks, getting tan, watching porn, ordering out. It was heaven. He tingled to think. Then one evening what's-his-name brought home a hustler. That totally pissed Henry off for some reason. What's-his-name and the hustler raped, then tried to strangle him. He flipped out, slashed an Impressionist painting worth millions of dollars. The hustler grabbed the knife, tried to stab Henry. He broke away, ran outside, waved down a car. The next day he woke up on his parents' front lawn with a couple of shallow stab wounds in his chest and a bruise necklace.

"Shi-i-i-it." Henry raised up too quickly or something. He had to grab onto the frame of the mirror and burp, burp, burp . . . Sweat dribbled out of his haircut and wound down his face in veiny patterns.

When the basement stopped whirling around, he realized how much he loved living there. Too bad there wasn't a way to leave and enter without going up through his parents' house. He'd often imagined a craggy, human-sized slot in the cinder block wall between the clock and TV, or, wait . . . Now that he thought of it, how about right here? The mirror could be the door. He'd glue a silver doorknob about an inch from the edge of the glass or Mylar or whatever this shiny stuff was.

He stood there a few seconds, skin bristling at the thought. He raised one arm and sort of studied a few of the zillions of tiny white peaks that had sprouted all over him. The sight made him feel weirdly tense and unliked for some reason.

"Fuck this." Henry pulled up his jeans, jammed his hand into their front left pocket, came back with a wadded-up

plastic bag. He swallowed whatever the fuck was inside it.
Seven yellow pills, courtesy of Craig.

He loped up the stairs, down a hall, froze, backed up three
steps, and looked to his right. "Weird." He leaned in the
doorway, appreciating the first little signs of whatever the pills
were about to compose. So far there was only a slight glowing.
But it helped him realize that the room where his parents were
sitting was pretty much the same shape as his basement, if
obviously scarier and less interesting to think about.

Ring.

"I'll get it!" Henry tore down the hall, grabbed the telephone. "Hi. Henry speaking."

"Hey, H., did you take those pills yet?" Craig asked in his
crumbly, stoned voice. It made him sound more cute and
friendly than he was.

"A few seconds ago."

"Oh, yeah? Wait an hour. That's how long ago I took my
stuff and I can't even pick up the phone. I'm on the floor . . .
and . . . and . . . and I'm like lying on the receiver. My head's
on top of it. I had to, like . . . this is unbelievable. I had to pull
the phone off the table by the cord and drag the thing to me,
like in those commercials of old people dying of heart attacks?
When they could have been saved by wearing little microphones around their necks?"

"Oh, shit."

"What?"

"Nothing. It's just that I'm going out. That guy Julian
called. I agreed to go fuck with his boyfriend and him."

"You planning to drive?"

"I was going to, but—"

"Listen, I'm, you won't, you wouldn't believe this . . . I'm so
fucked up. The *phone* is soft. It feels *soft* . . ."

Henry scrunched up his face, calculating the time it would
take to get the car, not to mention himself, across town.

"Craig, look, shut up for a second. When did you start not being able to move or whatever?"

"Just now before I called. It's getting scary. God, the room feels bad . . . uh, thick. It's kind of hard to breathe. You . . . you remember my poster of Joni Mitchell at Woodstock? It's, I mean it looks like she's under . . . I think it's . . . asphalt."

"Craig, I need to find Julian before this thing happens to me." He hung up the phone. Keys, he thought, and patted the lump in his front right pants pocket. "Okay, okay, okay . . ." He ran out the front door.

Unlocking the car was no problem. Starting was . . . different. The key looked like a jewel. Its design was incredibly intricate. He couldn't stop studying it, even when it was plugged in. It seemed a million times more relevant to his car than the lines on the freeway.

Blur.

He slumped in the driver's seat by a mansion, hopefully Julian's, wondering if the lock on the passenger door was down or up. He tried to compare his lock, which was definitely up, with the passenger one, but since his lock was closer, it would seem taller in any case. "Shit." He swung himself out the door, kicked it shut.

He teetered around. One hand clutched a chilly bouquet of the ivy that poured off the mansion's roof. His other hand jabbed at a dot on some antique molding that helpfully framed the out-of-focus front door. Once, twice . . .

(muffled) *Ding, dong.*

"Listen, Henry," he slurred. "Don't . . . fucking . . . talk." He tried to read his watch. "Jesus!" He held it right up to his eye. "Why the fuck . . . did I buy one of these pieces of shit with no numbers on it?"

Cre-e-e-eak.

The interior looked immense, dim, though yellowed by lamps in a few ornate spots. Far inside, or maybe not so far, stood a noisy silhouette. It was criticizing the way he looked, Henry felt almost sure. Another silhouette, more to Henry's left, added comments but they weren't as harsh. Besides, that one was whispering, whereas the farther one shouted. People didn't whisper cruel things, to Henry's knowledge.

"Hi, I . . . oops." He'd tripped on the doormat or something, but one of the silhouettes grabbed his shirt sleeve midfall. "Thanks, uh . . ." *Rustle.* A chilly hand slid past the band of his underwear. It started digging around in his ass. "I'm sorry, I know my crack is kind of hairy," he whispered, "but . . ." He remembered the party. It seemed to revolve in his mind around Julian hugging him. The guy seemed so sensitive then. He glanced over his shoulder, saw a pale, blurry face. Then he squinted and blinked at the other guy, me. I was still too far away, badly lit. The effort to see me made Henry's eyes water and sting so much he practically punched himself out trying to dry them off.

"Look, either don't talk at all," Julian said, rolling Henry over, "or try to say something hot about us, okay?" Henry murmured a word, but the drugs had eroded it. "Because you're exactly our type. You don't have to prove yourself." I splayed my hands on Henry's ass and pressed down, like he was lying in front of Grauman's Chinese Theater. The crack opened up. Julian cleared his throat, hocked some milky spit. Using his nails, he combed spit evenly through the hairs down there, reorganizing them into a spiral around the knotty, purple hole. "Yow," he said, curled his lip, "this guy's wild."

Julian positioned his thumbs to either side of the hole, yanked. It flew wide open. One of my ears squashed against one of his. He and I peered into the glittering well. "It's kind of unbelievably beautiful," I said. "Yeah, in a weird sense," Julian whispered. "It also reminds me of something, but I can't think what." My head lowered an inch, two, three.

"Poor guy," I muttered. Julian thought I looked psycho. "How so?" I just shrugged. "Oh, because it makes me want to fuck him over even more for some reason."

"Mmm." Julian slid two fingers into the ass. Henry's arms, which had laid very limp and nondescript to this point, started snaking around on the rug. A hand found Julian's knees and squeezed one of them twice. "Spooky," I said. The asshole had puffed up around Julian's knuckles. It made him think of that famous fur tea cup. "When I met this guy," he whispered, "I'd never, *ever* have guessed he was so out to lunch." He worked the fingers loose, wiping them on his calves. "But let's hurry before he gets sober and opinionated or whatever."

I crawled toward Henry's head. Julian reopened the asshole, spit, pushed in his cock, let the ass close around it. "Mmm." He looked up. I was eyeing the part in Henry's hair, or that general vicinity. "What?" Julian asked. "Oh, no big deal." I grinned. "It's just the way his hair's fallen into his face, and how straight the hair is, makes his head look like a lamp shade." Julian couldn't quite picture that. "I'm assuming this dent here's his mouth," I added, arching my hips. "Unh." A wrinkle appeared in my forehead. "Oh, *yeah*." My head toppled back.

Julian: "Let's trade." My head raised. "What? Sure, yeah, fine." Julian crawled up the body's right side, and I crawled down the left. Once he'd molded his lower half to Henry's shoulders and neck, with the head on his lap, Julian could see what I'd meant about the lamp shade. He pointed his cock at the wettest spot. It slid through the black folds. "Mmm." Then he noticed me lying facedown in the ass, eyes unfocused, my cheeks inflating, deflating . . . "Dennis?" Julian cocked his head. Nothing. "Dennis?!" He snapped his fingers . . .

. . . Julian figured out a way to lift Henry's face fairly high in the air, then drop it onto his cock, which would end up somewhere in the neck. That felt unbelievable. Plus, each up-down motion had a delayed, peculiar effect on Henry's ass.

The cheeks would cave in, then reinflate like lungs, giving Julian goosebumps and, from the look of it, making the route to the anus more pretty and treacherous for me. Even the guy's back improved. The homely spine and rib cage got swallowed up by the crazy pattern of his musculature or whatever . . .

. . . "Can you rim me? Are you in any condition . . . ?" Julian held one ear about an inch up from Henry's mouth. The guy was breathing, but it seemed a little too gentle and fragrant somehow, more like smoke. Julian sat back and squinted at me. "What if he OD's?" I was licking the guy's toes. "It's weird how . . . when feet are a little dirty . . . they're spicy," I said between licks. "But are they cold?" Julian asked. I quit licking. "Oh, I get it. Well, er, slap the guy." Julian aimed one palm, smacked Henry's cheek. "Hey," Henry groaned, "what the . . . fucking . . ."

. . . "Is he hard?" Julian asked. "Can you . . . reach down?" Most of my face disappeared behind Henry's ass, and tilted ninety degrees like a sinking ship. "Uh, no, not even close. It feels, what . . . squishy, rubbery?" I raised up. "Have you ever noticed," Julian said, his voice shaky from fucking the guy's mouth so hard, "how people don't get erections with us? Is it that the type we respond to is sort of asexual or something?" I pursed my lips. "Yeah, it's weird not to swallow their sperm." Julian shrugged. "I intend to, abstractly," he said, "but all I ever think about is dumping mine." . . .

. . . Henry stank, worse or better depending on where Julian licked. He'd had so much sex he could rank body odors. Asshole, profound. Crotch, overrated. Mouth, profound. Hair on head, underrated. Hands and feet, nice. Armpits, too blatant. Julian settled down on the ass. My face was wedged between Henry's thighs, pupils dilated, open mouth stuffed with wrinkly balls. "Mmm." Julian kissed me, imprisoning the balls, which he jabbed with the tip of his tongue. Occasionally I batted one back, as if it were the "ball" in a very crude sport . . .

... "Take control, yeah?" Julian let Henry go. The body toppled against me, slid down. I caught it. Hair was stuck to the sweat on Henry's face in ugly, hippieish patterns. Julian reached under the glass coffee table, grabbed the guy's discarded Adidas, unlaced one, threw it over his shoulder. He gathered and tied the locks into a tight ponytail. "Better," he said, sitting back on his heels. "Definitely. He's almost perfect now. Hmm. Eliminate one, two . . . two scars, some body hair, an eighth-inch around each nipple . . . maybe a little less nose . . . uh . . ." Julian squinted.

TENSE

1969–1986

When I was thirteen . . .

Saturday afternoons I'd ride my ten-speed downtown and
see matinees, usually horror films. I can't remember their
names anymore, since they were never the point of my
trips. I'd tune in, then recount their plot twists to my
parents at dinner to explain how I'd wasted my day. But as
soon as the credits rolled I'd be outside, hunched over,
unchaining my bike.

A couple of blocks off the main boulevard in a row of
Salvation Army–styled junk shops was a nondescript store-
front called Gypsy Pete's, full of sex magazines, run by an old,
unshaven alcoholic. Pete kept a few comic books near the
register for kids. But when the usual customers cleared out,
he'd let me browse through the hard-core material. I'd be
looking at two naked, tangled adults. Suddenly Pete would

yell, "Hey, twerp," which was the prearranged signal for me to return to the comics.

Pete used to talk drunkenly about how many women he fucked and how easily. I didn't believe him because he was ugly. He swore he'd been cute as a teen. One day he showed me a picture of him in the army or something in which he looked better but not good enough to get laid very much.

I thought he'd throw me out if I got near the gay porn, confined to a sleek, revolving rack near the register. So I'd browse in that area, glancing occasionally at the things on the rack. If I hung around long enough, Pete would go into the store's little toilet to shit. Those were my minutes to flip through the magazines. Once I thought Pete was heading off for his usual shit, but he was just taking something new out of the stockroom. I got caught with my hand on a copy of *Muscular Boy*. He didn't blink. "Skin's skin" was his philosophy.

Pete trusted me since I nodded along to his bull. So he started to show me the gay stuff before putting it on the rack. For the most part this stuff starred young hustler types, heavily tattooed, being fucked behind little black rectangles. Some dispensed with the rectangles. In a few, hustlers were tied up. Other hustlers, sometimes johns, pawed their crotches and spanked them while they pretended to scream.

Each Saturday Pete would produce a few new articles and let me sit in the stockroom with them for as long as I liked. At some point I realized he meant I could jerk off in peace, so I usually would, with a magazine spread on my knees, left hand holding a Kleenex, right hand turning the pages or jerking myself.

It stayed so dark in that stockroom I couldn't tell what time it was. Sometimes I'd be there for hours and not know. He'd yell, "Closing, twerp," which meant it was eight o'clock. I'd pedal home and tell my furious parents I liked the movie so much I'd stayed to see it a third or fourth time.

I was having sex with other kids by this point. None let me tie them up, but I remember one boy would hold his ankles together, pretending I'd captured him. Then I could spank him extremely lightly until he confessed some sort of secret, such as . . . Oh, who cares anymore.

One day Pete asked if I liked the slapping and spanking parts of the magazines best. I said yeah (and I actually did), so he pulled out more violent things, with nipple clamps, handcuffs, and dildos being standard equipment. Normal sex acts had disappeared from these shots. Still, I didn't complain in case he was hoarding items that held some new, even sexier world of . . . whatever.

I don't think Pete was after me physically. He never barged in. If he needed something out of the storeroom, he'd stand outside and yell, "Entering," then give me a couple of seconds to zip up or wipe myself off before he lifted the curtain that separated our worlds.

The last time I stopped by, Pete acted upset. Usually he'd make a few lame innuendos, pull out a new batch of stuff, and toss it over the counter to me. This time he started to say something, paused, muttered to himself. I didn't know what to do, so I wandered around the store seeing which magazines had been bought and which hadn't.

Pete motioned me to return to the front. "I have something to show you," he said. "But I don't know if I should." He squinted. "How old are you?" He'd always told me to tell any customer who might ask that I was eighteen, so that's how I answered. "No, no," he said, "I mean really." I told him I was thirteen. He closed his eyes for a second, swore, then asked me very slowly, like someone was forcing him, "Do you want to see items that might scare you a little?" I'd just seen a creature from outer space tear apart buildings, etc., so I said sure.

I followed him into the stockroom. I sat in the usual piss-smelling armchair. He reached up on one of the shelves and brought down a small stack of photos. Before he handed them to me he said, "If you don't understand these, we can talk. I'll be . . ." He pointed at the curtain, dropped the photo set into my lap. I looked up. I was totally alone and the curtain was settling back into place.

I didn't understand what was happening in the pictures at first, but after three or four I realized that the model was dead and not laughing or yelling like I'd originally thought. He was lying faceup on a bed. His wrists and ankles were tied with heavy rope, and there was a rope around his neck that I imagined had killed him. His eyes and his mouth were wide open. That's why I'd thought he was laughing. He was pale, cute, and had long, straight black hair. There was nobody else in the photos with him.

In the last couple of photos somebody had rolled the boy over, so we could see what he looked like on both sides, I guess. That's when I knew for sure he was dead because instead of an asscrack, he had a crater. It looked as if someone had set off a bomb in his rectum.

I studied the crater calmly for a minute or two before it shocked me. Then I set down the photos extremely gently. I parted the curtain, walked down an aisle and out the front of the store without speaking to Pete, because I couldn't. I remember Pete came to the doorway and stood there fidgeting, watching me unchain my bike. I climbed on, pedaled off. When I was about a half block down the street, I heard him yell, "Wait," then, "Stop that boy," like he thought, or else wanted people to think, that I'd stolen something.

When I was seventeen . . .

My boyfriend Julian worked in a gay massage parlor called Selma's. For something like a hundred dollars plus tip he'd

have sex with a client, the wilder or more complex the pro-
posed activity, the bigger Julian's tip. Being eighteen, adven-
turous, and pretty, he raked it in. That and the money I'd steal
from my parents kept us in drugs and alcohol most of that
summer.

Julian had slitty brown eyes, big lips, and the tip of his nose
turned up. Brown hair, shoulder length. He was slender, bony,
and his skin was the color of steamed glass. He owned about
three hundred different T-shirts, most of them printed with
rock bands' or products' names. Jeans or cut-offs. Tennis
shoes, no socks. I dressed in a similar style, but my hair's
wavy, and just sort of clogs up when I grow it out. I was four
inches taller than Julian, which would put him at, say, five
foot eight and a half.

My only photo of Julian was shot by a client at Selma's.
He's gagged and tied up in a fetal position. His ass is covered
with flowery handprints. From the thighs down and rib cage
up, he's very fuzzy. Still, from what you can see of his face it's
obvious why someone would have paid to do something like
that to him.

One night we got totally fucked up on mescaline. Too high,
in fact, to go into the world. But you need stuff to do when
you're that drugged, so Julian phoned this cute hippie he'd
met and asked the guy to get stoned and have sex with us.

When Henry came by he was already so zonked on something we had to undress him, which made for some interesting sex, but there was a quality about him that nagged me the
whole time. I kept thinking I'd met him or that he was famous or . . . something. Eventually I figured it out. Henry
looked spookily like the model I'd seen with his asshole
blown open at Gypsy Pete's four years before. I started calculating right there, while we were eating him out, etc., how I
could ask.

Then Julian accidentally dropped Henry's forehead on the

edge of the coffee table. He wasn't hurt though, just confused for a second.

We'd pretty much figured him out, so when he said, "I'm not bleeding, but maybe I should split," Julian, acting as our spokesman, agreed. Henry was at the front door, negotiating the sill, when I managed to ask if he'd ever made pornos. I think Julian was in the kitchen or bathroom.

Henry stopped, wheeled around. "What do you mean by pornos?" He seemed sober all of a sudden.

"Magazines, photographs," I said. I grinned like it wasn't important whether he answered or not.

"Yeah, why?" He rested his weight on the doorframe.

I told him about the photos I'd seen of a boy with his asshole blown open.

Henry started grinning as soon as I mentioned the wound. "You saw those?" he said. "Really? I never saw those. Do you still have them, because . . . ?"

I shook my head, but I don't think he was paying attention to me at that moment. He looked very dazed and excited or something.

". . . Man, that's funny," he concluded.

I tried to look like I thought it was funny too. Maybe it was. "You seemed dead in them," I said.

"Oh, I used to do anything if somebody was nice to me. I was with that photographer guy for a while, and he took lots of pictures of me. I didn't know he was turning me into a business, at least not at first. Most of the shots were just me jerking off. I was stoned *all the time*. But those were bizarre, those dead ones."

Maybe because he was so overwrought, Henry looked different in some way—older, less sexy, but easier to be with. "Do you remember how you did it?" I asked. "I mean how you or the photographer made that wound look so real?"

"Wait," Henry said. "Describe the pictures to me because we did a bunch of different ones."

I did, very colorfully, the way I'd described the images to myself while jerking off. Spoken aloud, the descriptions seemed much more pretentious, ridiculous, amoral . . . something, than they'd ever been in the secret, uncritical world of my fantasies. But Henry didn't care how sexily I described the idea of him dead. He just listened and nodded like I was giving him directions to the next town.

"It was makeup," he said. "And I think some dyed cotton glued on, but I'm not sure because I was lying on my stomach, and it took him hours to get the thing right. Strange man, but nice. I was probably in love with him. In fact I'm sure I was." He smiled and shook his head, one of those funny-how-life-is shakes. "Anyway, I almost forgot. Shit. I'm going to ask you my standard question now, so get ready. Uh, if you could change one thing about the way I acted back when we were having sex, what would that be? Be honest." He grinned.

I thought for a second. "Well, I'd want you to be less stoned."

Henry shook his head. "Yeah, obviously. I mean besides that."

I couldn't think of anything. "No, I guess not."

"Oh, really? Thanks a lot. That's nice." He looked shocked. "So, uh, call me sometime," he said like he meant it, but I guess he didn't.

"I might." I think if he'd stayed or if I'd called him, maybe he could have answered some questions about those images that went on to completely direct or destroy my life in a way. That's what I've realized now. At the time I just waited for him to take off. Once he had, Julian and I compared notes.

*   *   *

When I was eighteen . . .

Julian moved to France with an older man he met at Selma's. Occasionally I'd get a postcard. Even before the move I'd started spending time with Julian's kid brother, Kevin, a devastatingly cute twelve-year-old with psychological problems. Julian had always kept a lot of distance from him for that reason.

Physically he was a Julian replica, only shorter, and sort of too pretty. He had this violent effect on me, something like comic book characters probably have on stoned kids. I'd fantasized drawing him into our sex life, despite his size and behavior, because he was outwardly perfect.

One day I'd hitchhiked over to visit Julian, as per routine. Kevin had answered the door. He said Julian was out. I asked what he, meaning Kevin, was up to. Nothing, he said, and led me dutifully up to his room.

The room was weird, almost empty apart from a bed and an overstuffed bookcase. I remember I asked about that. He said it was so he could redecorate in his head. That first day, for instance, he said the room had been a submarine stuck on the floor of the ocean, at least until I showed up. We talked about that and other stuff until Julian arrived a few hours later, drunk and rich.

After Julian moved away, I'd visit Kevin. We'd do drugs and talk, usually about Julian, whom Kevin admired to the point of psychosis, I thought, until one day I realized his love was more than familial. I tried to pin Kevin down. He eventually confessed to being "in love" with his brother, but claimed nothing had "happened" between them. To me the idea of them being in love was erotic. So I kept steering our repartee back to his Julian fantasies, which were incredibly sketchy as I recall.

One day Kevin's mom called me up to say how happy she was about my friendship with Kevin, whom she'd "written off" after Julian left. He seemed more stable since knowing me, she said. In fact he'd told her he loved me as much as he'd ever loved Julian, which she thought was kind of sweet, I guess.

I drove right over. When he answered the door I said I wanted to fuck him. He hugged me all the way up the staircase, down the hall, into his room. I kicked the door shut, and kind of shoved him against it. His throat made a sound I'd never heard before. It was high-pitched, loud. At the same time his legs buckled. I saw the pre-collapse tremors, threw my arms around his waist, and just managed to hold him upright by the seat of his jeans. I walked him to the bed, dropped his body across it. He wouldn't let go of my shirt and tore a huge hole.

Technically, he was a know-nothing. He kept toppling or being knocked off the bed, scratching his elbows, knees, bruising things, spraining his arms, back, etc. After a month he got so much less attractive I had to imagine I'd just rescued him from a rapist, or was raping him myself, to get involved in the sex. He never knew, though.

If I had to describe Kevin using one word I'd say hysterical. It seemed to have something to do with insecurity, but he kept freaking out all the time, even after I spent hours trying to convince him I loved him, which I'd started to do, according to my loose, personal definition of that word.

Still, it's weird how removed I became from those problems. I mean, I've gotten totally removed from almost everyone now, as far as I can tell, but with him I surprised myself because I was still just a typical person at that point, I think. Being cold was the only way I could deflect all his . . . emotion, whatever. I'm repeating myself.

*   *   *

When I was twenty-four . . .

I wore black, cut my hair, dyed it black, took a lot of amphetamines, and renamed myself Spit. My second home was a punk club called Flintstones, housed in the shell of a pizza joint Julian and I had occasionally haunted. I went there on the weekends to look for somebody to love. That was a very unpunk thing to think about, but people did. I just acted on it.

I found Samson swaying around on the dance floor, separated from me by some pogo-ing kids. He was thin, tallish, big boned, with a perky Scandinavian face a little muddied by freckles and zits. His hair was dyed blue-black and stiffened with gel into twelve-inch-long strands, most of which were bunched up on the top of his head like a scorched bouquet.

When I met his eyes and imitated their unfocused stare he seemed to recognize something and stumbled in my direction.

He had an apartment nearby, one huge single room with seven double beds scattered around "for friends." The floor was an inch deep in handbills, underwear, T-shirts . . . He stood in the middle and yanked off his shirt. I flopped on a random bed. His chest was a little too narrow and pockmarked. It was all information to me.

He unsnapped his jeans and pushed them halfway down the shaft of his cock before he stopped, grinned at it, then at me.

"When you only see this part," he slurred, pointing at the visible part of his cock, "you figure what's next is total godhead, right, Spit? But when you see what you get . . ." And he yanked down the jeans. They slid as far as his knees. "It's so ugly, the whole thing." He picked up the trio and shook them roughly. "Especially the cock." He held it up. "*Ug*-ly."

I told him something like, Hey, it's exactly the ugliness or whatever that makes cocks paradoxical and invaluable, blah

blah blah, especially on really cute boys like himself. I said it suggested depth, poetry, seriousness . . . I could be really pretentious back then.

He made a face like he didn't know what I was talking about, though he later confessed that the word "cute" is what helped him waddle toward me, jeans inching down his calves.

I grabbed his ass, pulled him close, sucked his cock, licked his balls, etc., while in the blurry upper edge of my vision his head wobbled and drooled like a surrealistic cloud.

Let's see . . . It was weeks later. I'd started to drift off a lot during sex, which Samson didn't particularly notice. In reality I was caressing him. In my head I'd be grabbing objects off the night table, crushing his skull, then mutilating his body, especially his ass, while he tried to dissuade me from murdering him in a brain-damaged voice.

I used to worry that ideas like those would show up on my face, but it's too crude to register anything wilder than "I'm feeling happy" or "sad" or "pissed off" or "horny" or "scared."

One night I got Samson so loaded he walked like the carpet was quicksand or something. He couldn't speak, I don't think. I aimed him at the bed, where he fell. I knelt over his chest and gazed down at his face until it blurred. Then I punched it. Again. I sort of lost my way, I can't remember exactly. Things were breaking. Sometimes I'd catch one of Samson's eyes studying me, which I guess was a muscle reflex.

I should include some reaction shots here, I know, but I doubt I had many. I felt numb, blank, so my face probably followed suit. When the incident's over, *long* over, I'll try to sort out the boy and myself from the violence and feel anything. I'm not at that point yet.

For weeks afterward I expected police to show up at my apartment. When they didn't, I figured Samson was still alive but too mentally ruined to name names, or else his body was still sprawled there, rotting away, and nobody had missed him enough to check in.

One night I was drinking at Flintstones. The decor of that club was extravagant, a pseudo-cave with lifelike plaster stalactites and puddles of fake stagnant water. I was admiring it for the millionth time when I saw Samson pogo-ing a few yards away. There were still some bruises and cuts on his face, but since punks wore their physical damage like fashion accessories, he didn't particularly stand out.

I tried to disappear, but on my way to the exit our eyes accidentally met. I nodded, not knowing what else to do. He stopped dancing, held up one finger, as if to say, "Wait," then went back to his pogo-ing. First I froze. Then I moved out of the traffic flow and watched him gyrate. He didn't look angry. If anything, he seemed happier or something. Maybe I just saw him more sharply than before, since beauty wasn't distracting me. Or maybe I'd damaged some nerves, and his face had fewer directions to go in.

When the song ended, he strolled over. "God, Spit, the last time I saw you was so fucking strange." He grinned crookedly. "I was *so* out of it. And you were *so* weird."

I wanted to know what happened after I left.

"At first I was scared," he said. His face seemed confused, but there were too many new little wrinkles and details to tell. "I couldn't decide if I should go to the emergency room. Then I thought, Fuck it. I laid around, took drugs, watched TV, and pigged out for a month. It was fun. That's why I'm fat, if you noticed."

I said I had, now that he mentioned it. Then I asked if it bothered him.

"No way, Spit." He shook his head, then stopped, nodded. "Well, it did at first, okay, sure." He laughed, which made his scars really stand out. "But it was weird being cute. It's not as great as you think." He took a swallow of beer and leaned back on the wall of the cave. "So, no." Then his eyes got this icy, removed look I sort of expect in the people I fuck. "Not anymore."

When I was twenty-eight . . .

After I lost it with Samson, I spent a few years avoiding serious, ongoing relationships as a precaution. The few times I had sex were one-night affairs with guys I'd never have to run into again. Mostly hustlers.

The hustler I remember best for some reason was a thin, heavy-metal-style teen standing along the so-called porn strip, a few city blocks not far from my apartment. He grabbed the crotch of his jeans as I drove by. I swerved to the curb. He ran up to the passenger window, leaned in. I asked if he wanted to "party." He named his price (I forget), I agreed, he joined me, we drove off.

He was almost exactly my type. The only flukes were his neck, which was quite long and thin, a crooked nose crusty with snot, and he may have had one lazy eye. He said his name was Finn. I had him spell it. He said he got that nickname because when he was younger he'd either resembled or acted like Huckleberry Finn. I said it was obviously "acted like" since his namesake was just a character in a book. But Finn said his copy had illustrations.

It wasn't that I didn't fantasize murdering hustlers. It's just that I tend to be too scared or shy the first few times I sleep with someone to do what I actually want. The worst that could, and did, happen was I'd get a little too rough. But the hustler would stop me, or I'd stop myself, before things became more than conventionally kinky, as far as he knew.

My perfect type tends to be distant, like me. I don't mean

matter-of-fact, I mean shut tight. Like he's protecting himself from other people or pain or both by excising himself from the world in every way, apart from the obvious physical stuff you need to get by such as walk, talk, eat, etc.

All the way home I kept turning to look at Finn's face. It was almost beautiful. He didn't even notice me studying, he was so uninterested or overly involved in himself.

Usually I'd offer hustlers a beer. We'd sit around, lie to each other, but as soon as I let Finn inside he asked, "Where's the toilet?" When he came out of the toilet, he said, "Let's get this over with." I'm trying to remember his voice. I just can't. He found my bedroom all by himself, and the bed, even though there was no light at all. Even I had some trouble negotiating the furniture and stuff.

I felt around on the bed until my hand held a foot. I sat down next to it. I rubbed it for a while, wondering what to do, say. AIDS was an issue by then, so I'm pretty sure I said I wanted to turn on the lamp and examine him, period, to which he relaxed or moved his foot in a way I understood to mean "fine" or "who cares?"

I flicked on a lamp and knelt over Finn's nude body. The smell off of him was intense, like leaning over a barbeque, only more subtle and hard to describe. I mean sweet, but kind of spoiled. Like there was something wrong with him, hidden away in there.

Finn was thin, tall, pale. He had so few hairs on his legs that I counted them. His buttocks were springy as balloons. His asshole looked like a photo I saw of a bullet hole. He had big, red, droopy balls. His cock was thin with a pointy head. Black pubic hair, thick and smelly. His ribs almost pierced through his chest and back. His nipples were tiny pink matterhorns. He was warm all over except for his ass, hands, and feet, which were freezing. If you held out his arms at a particular angle you could fit tennis balls into his underarm cavities, they were so deep and round. His face was bluish-white with brown eyes that seemed one thought behind or ahead of me constantly. Full red lips, nicotine-stained teeth, huge mouth, beer breath.

I went over his body once more to make sure I got everything right. He was silently jerking off, squinting up at the ceiling, forehead rippled down the middle. I'd been hard all along without touching myself, but when I finished my study I started to jerk my cock. I inched forward until it was hanging over his chest. I think I imagined that we were on top of an Aztec pyramid. I held a knife or whatever they used in those days to sacrifice Finn to whoever they thought they worshiped back then.

I couldn't sustain an illusion like that for more than a second or two, so I came on his chest, with a groan I'm sure. Then I leaned back and caught my breath, watching the splatters of sperm run together. The lacy pattern they formed reminded me of those tacky vests gays used to wear at the height of the disco craze. That totally wiped out the last of my lust.

Finn stopped jerking himself, closed his eyes, and lay there in the rumpled sheets, letting my sperm dry all over him.

I'd seen what I wanted to see and went into the toilet to wash off my cock in the basin. When I looked up one time I saw Finn behind me in the mirror, waiting his turn, I guess.

Part of me wanted to kill and dismember him, which I probably could have done without getting arrested, but most of me gave him a towel, then humored him until he left.

Afterward I lay in bed putting Finn through hell in my thoughts. I tore up his body like it was a paper bag and pulled out dripping fistfuls of veins, organs, muscles, tubes. I made his voice as otherworldly as civil defense sirens had sounded to me as a kid. I drank his blood, piss, vomit. I shoved one hand down his throat, one hand up his ass, and shook hands with myself in the middle of his body, which sounds funny, but it wasn't.

When I was thirty . . .

The detours around AIDS weren't marked yet. A lot of guys my age, even younger, were testing positive, sick, dead. Samson (I went to his funeral), a lot of friends and fucks I haven't mentioned, (according to the rumor mill) Henry. I avoided sex, no matter how tentative, talked on the phone, and occasionally had drinks with a few male friends—predators and aesthetes like me, as opposed to "my type."

One of these friends, Samuel, an actor, although he'd never actually been in any movies or plays, had grown romantically obsessed with this clerk at the Sears where he worked part-time. When Samuel described Joe one day, I got obsessed secondhand. Not only did Joe meet my strict physical requirements (pale, thin, smooth, dark hair, dark eyes, big lips, spaced-out, boyish), but his only passion, as far as Samuel could tell, was splatter films such as *A Nightmare on Elm Street*, etc. In other words, Joe seemed so right I got sloppy. I told Samuel, If you don't click with Joe, please play Cupid. He hemmed, hawed, agreed.

Eventually Samuel seduced the boy. I'd been trying to downplay my interest, but when Samuel called one night, post-sex, disappointed because Joe turned out to be this extremely serious masochist, I insisted he introduce us. He said he would, though he'd already passed Joe the telephone number of some character actor who was notoriously sadistic in bed.

Samuel spent much of the weekend coaching me with Joe trivia so I could waltz into Sears the following Tuesday and meet him, totally primed. Tuesday morning Samuel called. Hold off, he said. Joe hadn't shown up for work. A week passed, no Joe. A month, two.

One day there was a sketch in the newspaper of a seemingly pretty young man. Cops had found an anonymous, dismembered corpse in the yard of that very character actor. They asked for anyone who recognized this conjectural portrait (apparently drawn from the corpse) to contact them. Samuel said it looked a little like Joe, he couldn't be sure, and I'm not sure the cops ever figured out who the corpse was.

The case was perfect fodder for my interest in sexual death. I grew obsessed for a year, following it through the media, researching Joe's life via friends of friends, filling in blanks with my own fantasies. I even spent several months trying to channel the info I'd gathered into an artsy murder-mystery novel, some salvageable fragments of which are interspersed through the following section.

TORN

1986 (1987)

Thursday night, Friday morning

Joe pried up the trapdoor. He crouched, aimed a flashlight beam into his basement. The view was milky with cobwebs, so he kicked a hole. That framed the top several rungs of a rope ladder. He studied them for a few seconds, shrugged, and jumped into the black.

Thud.

He ran his light over the concrete walls, found a few nails where tools used to hang. Now there were shadows of saws, hammers, wrenches. A wooden shelf held some crumbly newspapers. He riffled through. They spewed ticklish dust. "Ah-ah-ah-ah-ah—choo!" Between two comics sections somewhere near the base of the pile, he spied the buttocks-shaped end of a large, white bone. When he drew the thing out, it was sixteen, seventeen, eighteen inches long.

"Hmm." He forced one end of the bone into the back pocket of his faded jeans.

The floor of the basement was empty, apart from some waterlogged, mass-market paperbacks off in a corner. Soft-core porn, detective novels, sci-fi, etc. He razed a garish stack with one kick.

Climbing the rope ladder, he tried to imagine his skeleton folding and straightening out inside his skin, but his knowledge of bodies was slight, and his brain such a weakling it couldn't conceptualize a crisp image.

The phone rang. His answering machine picked up. It was his friend Samuel, who mentioned switching on channel 9. Joe laid the bone on the dining room table. Dropping into an armchair, he reached out and snagged the remote control unit.

An old man was strangling a boy. He winced, squealed, gulped, pleaded. A shorter old man held a knife an inch or two from the boy's chest. It was sporting an Iron Maiden T-shirt. The men laughed and eyeballed each other. One winked. Then the shorter man shoved the blade into Iron Maiden's intricate logo.

Joe opened his eyes after what felt like seconds but could have been hours. The cigarette had burned out. At the spot where its nub came to rest on the fabric, smoke rose in a wavering column. Far off, his TV set framed some completely uninteresting static.

He slapped the smoldering arm, switched off the TV, headed upstairs, and caught a few hours of actual sleep in his bed.

When his coffee got cold the next morning he studied the bone he'd found, occasionally rubbing his own bones by way of comparison. It almost matched the size and shape of the one in his forearm. Still, his seemed a little less round. Hard to tell through the padding and shit. He squeezed his shoulders. Their bones were overly complicated. He felt down his body. Ribs, too flat and delicate. There was nothing

particularly worthwhile in his waist, as far as he could sur-
mise, so he skipped to his hips, which reminded him of a
Möbius strip.

Pushing his Jockey shorts down to his knees, he started
studying the hipbone, digging into its hollows and nooks with
his fingertips. He bent over, spread his legs, knelt, squatted . . .
He'd never realized how inventive his skeleton could be. It had
just been in storage inside him for twenty-six years, like a
piece of unfashionable sculpture.

He pulled up his shorts, hit the kitchen, dumped chilly
coffee, and washed out the cup.

Trotting back down the hall he punched PLAY on his phone
machine. Samuel's message played again, only this time he
sounded depressed. Shit, Joe thought, glancing up at the clock.
8:47.

Rrrring, click. "Hello?" Samuel said groggily.

"It's me." Joe despised his own voice. It was too deep or
something. No matter how he distorted it, it had the fake
homeyness of those DJs announcing classical music or soft
rock.

"Oh, Joe. Hi. You got my message? Did you catch anything
of that show I mentioned?"

"I'm not sure," Joe said. "I sort of fell asleep."

"Too bad." Samuel snorted. "That actor you look like,
Keanu Reeves, was getting physically fucked up by psycho-
paths."

"How come?"

"How come what?"

"How come they fucked him up?"

"*I* don't know, who cares," Samuel muttered, yawned.
"Obviously because he was *so fucking cute.*"

Joe yawned, eyed the greasy brown clock face set into his
distant stovetop. 8:53. "Bye. I'll see you at work."

Click.

*   *   *

(I'm writing this en route from LAX to Kennedy Airport. I must be insane to just take off. But I'm famous for this kind of shit. And for not thinking thoroughly. That's my friends' problem, not mine. Jealousy, that's what their idiocy is about. I'm more "experienced" than any of them. I've imagined scenes they couldn't even start to think up. And one of the things that goes on when you mentally explore a certain area of life like I do is you start to understand all of it. Or else you know exactly what you want out of it, and the rest doesn't matter. For me this want begins with a physical type. Over the years I've decided or figured out that there's a strain of the human race I'm uncontrollably drawn to. Male, younger, lean, pale, dark-haired, full-lipped, dazed looking. I think the lineage stretches back to those pictures of Henry at Gypsy Pete's. He, or they, were the original. Every guy I've wanted since has had his same basic look. I suppose in a sense it's like being involved with the same person over and over without getting bored. That's how I think of it. Anyway, it's the closest I'll get to a long-term relationship. But finding cooperative guys isn't easy, at least since I've grown so obsessed with the idea of murdering someone. That's the area of life I was hinting at earlier. And that's why I'm flying to NYC. I keep thinking about this boy Pierre Buisson who I recently saw in a porn video, *All of Me*. He's the most perfect human being I've seen since, well, Kevin at least. Like most porn stars these days he's a hustler on the side. Available. Through a particular escort service advertised in *The Advocate*. In New York. Without the mess of real relationships. Let me say before I go on that everything I do is based on an urge that I don't understand, though I keep trying to understand it.)

Friday morning

Sears had been painted light purple a month, six weeks back. That was supposed to attract a younger clientele. Instead it seemed to antagonize regulars. Joe's station was empty, apart from a few figures lingering along the border of Men's Wear and Home Entertainment. He leaned on a cash register and was quickly sucked in by an image on one of the distant TVs.

A muscular man with a flattop was holding a gun on some teenaged boys. They didn't care. They sneered and yelled things until the man fired, so many shots, even when they were sprawled on the ground, that there was obviously lots of psychological baggage concealed by the set's lack of volume.

"Great, huh?" said a nasal voice. Joe glanced at Samuel, who was hanging around in an aisle near Joe's station, straightening stacks of blue jeans. Lately he'd gotten so tan he looked Mexican. "The film," Samuel added, nodding at the distant, rectangular image.

"Think so?" Joe said cautiously. Samuel had one of those voices that could have been dripping with irony or totally serious. Who knew? "Hmm, well . . ." He noticed a customer standing a few aisles away. ". . . Yeah, great, uh, excuse me a sec?"

Joe trotted off, holding his tie in place. Ten feet away from the customer, a short, red-haired man, he skidded to a stroll. "Hi," he smiled. "Need some help?"

The redhead looked up from the One-Half-Off rack, smiled toothily. "Couldn't hurt."

Joe suddenly had a mild déjà vu. It whited out his view for a second.

"I want a nice shirt," the redhead continued through the clearing haze. "Not too elegant, but not . . . jarring."

That voice was so familiar, Joe thought, though more uncertain and/or high-pitched than usual. Obviously the guy was famous or something. "I'm a fan of your work," he mumbled, to see what would happen.

The redhead was stroking the sleeve of a bright yellow shirt with a cowboy-esque motif embroidered on the cuffs. He had predictably wee, freckled hands. "Is this silk?" he asked.

"Banlon," Joe said.

The redhead dropped the sleeve like it was scalding. He blew on his fingertips, and kept blowing until Joe realized he was supposed to respond, and laughed a little stiffly.

Satisfied or whatever, the redhead stuffed the sleeve back into the sleeve cliff.

Joe pretended to straighten the cliff up a bit. "Did you hear what I said?"

"Mm-hm. Thanks . . ." The redhead crossed his arms, eyed the plastic tag on Joe's pocket. ". . . Joe."

"No problem. Anyway, you must get harassed by fans like me all the time, I guess."

The redhead smiled toothily again. "Actually, most people don't take my kind of acting that seriously, per se."

Actor, Joe thought. "Well, they're wrong . . ." He bullshit-ted for ten, fifteen seconds, hoping something would draw out the names of some movies or something. ". . . Anyway, what's next for you, I mean role-wise?" That should do it.

"This." The redhead shut his eyes, blanked out his freckly face. "Ready?" he whispered, not waiting for a reply. "Now." He smiled again. One hand shot upright and clenched, as though wielding a knife or sword. He jabbed "it" in Joe's general direction a few times. "Imagine you're . . . screaming . . . spurting blood," he said through clenched teeth.

Joe's cock hardened instantaneously. He was reaching down to conceal it when . . .

"You *wish*," Samuel sniffed from somewhere behind Joe. He'd joined them without either one noticing.

The redhead shoved his hands into his pants pockets, glanced at Joe's crotch, mumbled something to Samuel, and walked away without buying anything.

Joe could feel his cheeks burning. "Oh, hi, Samuel, uh . . ."

"Listen, Joe," Samuel whispered as soon as the redhead was out of earshot. He looked unusually emotional. "Watch your-self around Gary. I'm talking major sadist, okay? One time

this cute 'ex' of mine accidentally went home with him
and . . ."

Joe leaned close.

(We're over Kansas, for the record. It's flat with a few scattered buildings and roads. The interior of the plane is more
interesting. I don't mean the seats and stuff. I mean two rows
ahead of me there's a Belgian or Dutch family of various ages
and sexes, all clumped around one aisle seat, doting over its
occupant, a boy, maybe twenty. I just noticed them. He has a
great profile, sharp nose, full lips, big eyes, thick brown
bangs. That's all I've been able to see as of yet. But it's
enough. Weird how his family's fawning. He's my type, for
sure, but I know from experience that my type's not standard, though most people admit that my type's pretty hot.
Hmm. I'm in a window seat. There's no occupant on the
aisle. Across the aisle some older guy and his wife are tipped
back in their seats asleep. Great. See, I've gotten a hard-on
just based on this glimpse of the boy. And planes make
me horny in general, because they're so cramped or something. So I'm unzipping my jeans and removing my hard-on.
There, great. It's one of those inexplicable things. The more
I look at that pampered boy, the worse I want to do something intense to him. I don't like to use the word "sex"
because what I'm interested in is more serious, though it
resembles sex superficially. That's what happens when you're
so specific about the kind of partner you want. It's not just
hot stuff with cute guys who look vaguely alike. It means
perfecting your feelings for them, or dissecting their seem-
ing perfection, or . . . Shit. Like right now, if I could coerce
that boy into one of the jet's little toilets with me, I'd turn
psychotic, I'm sure. Actually, it's more like my body would
lose it, and I'd be observing the damage it does from a safe
place inside.)

Friday evening

Joe sprawled in Samuel's Datsun. They burned rubber. The freeway was empty. Occasionally one of Samuel's hands left the steering wheel, messed around with the crotch of Joe's slacks. Its wrinkles and creases would focus, unfocus, suggest other things, like a cloud did when viewers looked hard and long enough.

Honk, honk.

Samuel's apartment building was one of those beige stucco, two-story types rimmed with catwalks. He unlocked the door. 2E. Joe took a chair in the living room, hands folded casually in his lap. Samuel was hunched over next to a shiny mahogany cabinet mixing screwdrivers. Joe looked around at some artwork that didn't register.

Samuel handed him one of the drinks, clinked their rims. *Ding.*

"I know you like violence," Samuel said by way of a toast, "but does that mean you're into S&M?"

Joe was taking a drink, which he gulped down in order to answer. "Well . . ." he choked.

"Anything I'm interested in doing to you, basically?" Samuel smiled, took a sip.

Still choking, Joe waved his left hand to mean *Give me a second,* then looked up to see if Samuel had gotten the message.

Samuel leered, sipping.

Joe set down his glass and tried to cough out the burning. No luck. He doubled up. When he felt a fist pounding his back, he made his lips mime the phrase, "Thanks a lot." Samuel kind of waltzed him through the furniture, down a hall, accidentally scraping walls, into an unlighted room. That felt dramatic.

Slam.

"I'll be honest with you," whispered Samuel's voice. It was moving around in the dark like a ghost's.

"That's nice," Joe said, not particularly interested. His voice was still kind of raspy. He cleared his throat, pulled out a cigarette, lit up, took a drag. "There. Sorry about that." He belly-flopped on the bed, exhaled smoke. "Ready."

"Okay, um . . . here goes." Samuel's hands started scrunching and kneading the seat of Joe's slacks like they intended to sculpt something out of him. That felt okay, if a little monotonous. After a while they lifted.

"One second, yeah?" Joe stood, smashed his cigarette out in what he hoped was an ashtray, pushed his slacks and underwear to his knees, lay back down, and took a breath. "Go ahead."

The hands squeezed Joe's bare ass once, twice, froze there, then jerked away. "What am I feeling?" Samuel whispered. "Welts?"

Joe's cock hardened, maybe thanks to the shock in Samuel's voice. "Mm-hm."

"Is that what . . . ?"

"Afraid so."

". . . you're into . . ."

"Basically."

". . . because I don't know if I can . . ." Samuel slapped Joe's ass lightly. "Like this?" he squeaked, and spanked Joe again.

Joe rested his cheek on the knuckles of one hand and relaxed. *Slap.* His ass stung innocuously. Up his asshole the feeling was much more complex and kind of itchy. *Slap, slap.* It made Joe imagine a beehive. *Slap.* Still, he tried not to focus because any image would soften the blows. *Slap, slap, slap.* He had to be right in the middle of it. "Yeah. Right. Higher, harder." Etc. *Thud.* Joe felt a very dull pain in his lower back. *Thud.* Another pain higher up. By the third he could tell they were fists. Finally. *Thud . . . thud, thud.* Neck, ass, rib cage . . . The violence petered out. "What's up?" Joe squinted over his shoulder. Samuel's silhouette was just visible at the foot of the bed, hunched over in the dark, a Rodin. "Why'd you stop?" Joe thought he tasted blood. So he poked his tongue around inside his mouth in search of rough spots or dents. "I mean, that was great." He couldn't find anything wrong.

Samuel shook his head violently. "I'm . . . *very, very* . . . sorry."

"Look," Joe sighed. He arched his hips, tugging his slacks and shorts over them. "I guess I'm self-destructive. Except I don't see it that way. Because I tend to experience things, even weird things like violence, as forms of information about what or who I am physically." He finished zipping and snapping. "So don't think twice." He rolled over, grinned, snuck a glance at the bedside clock. 11:21. "Forget it ever happened, in fact." He held out his hand.

(Another thing about planes. When I'm stuck on one for several hours I tend to become more aware of myself from the neck down, probably because I'm so cramped in this seat. Usually I don't notice my body. It's just there, working steadily. I wash it, feed it, jerk it off, wipe its ass, and that's all. Even during sex I don't use my body that much. I'm more interested in other guys'. Mine just sort of follows my head and hands, like a trailer. I don't care if guys want to do things with it. Wait. Actually that stuff makes me very uncomfortable, unless I'm drunk. People I like must pick up on my tastes right away, since they almost never want to explore me. They just lie back, take it from me. But the way I'm contorted to fit in this seat makes my body ache. And it's strange to be forced to acknowledge my body exists because I'm sure I've neglected the thing for so long that it's totally fucked up and full of cancer or AIDS or something. Maybe if I stop writing this down, I'll stop worrying.)

(Later. They're starting the movie.)

Monday morning

The most interesting things in the office were charts showing human anatomy, one male, one female. Covering most of a wall, they showed lifesize, young-looking people whose flesh had been peeled off at various points. The purplish stuff inside the wounds made Joe think of a pair of pajamas he'd worn when he was seven, eight.

Crea-ea-ea-k.

Dr. Ashman, who'd been listening to a Walkman, oblivious, eyes scribbling on the ceiling, sat up and blinked at Joe. "*What* . . . are *you* doing *here?*"

"I'm scheduled for a physical," Joe said, a little startled. The doctor looked blank. "Joseph Evans." Nothing. "From Sears?"

"Oh, of course. Sorry." The doctor tore off his headphones, sticking them into a baggy white pocket. "I thought you were someone else." He picked up a clipboard, flipped through its slight stack of pages. "So I . . . see you've written here under medical history something about a . . . 'weird nervous system'?"

"Yeah." Joe nodded. "But I've got a question that's completely off the subject, if you've got a second."

Dr. Ashman squinted at his wristwatch. When he didn't look up, Joe guessed that meant go ahead. Joe slid the bone from the back pocket of his faded jeans, held it out. "I found this thing in my basement a few days ago. Is it human?"

The doctor took the bone, turned it over a few times, and squinted at the wall with the charts. "I think . . . ," he said, approaching the wall. He scanned the male figure. "No, I'm sure that it *is* human, yes. It's a tibia, or, in layperson's terms, the lower half of a leg. Here." He squeezed one of his calves.

Joe nodded. "Do you think somebody dismembered somebody?"

The doctor said something about that not being what he meant at all, but Joe couldn't quite hear. He was too busy staring off into the charts, fantasizing a guy about his age and looks, with one bone missing. The daydream burned off before he could build anyone in particular.

"Time." The doctor walked behind a partition, started washing his hands.

Joe took off everything but his underwear and hopped up onto the flimsy exam table, resting his eyes on the charts. The subjects' faces were a little too impish and sweet, but their skin looked realistic, if kind of colorless. He couldn't be sure if the visible parts of the skeleton and guts were correct. He hoped so, shivered.

The doctor reemerged, wiping his hands on a paper towel. His eyes froze on Joe's crotch, blinked, then darted over the rest of his body. "Do you . . . want to tell me about those?"

Joe thought for a second, shrugged.

"Does this hurt?" The doctor reached out, pushed a lumpy bruise near the ridge of Joe's pubic hair. That felt okay.

"Not really."

"Could you lie on your back for me?"

The doctor began to examine Joe, starting up at some outlying marks near the lightly scarred shoulders and working down his raggedy chest. The older man's eyes studied his the whole time, watching, Joe guessed, for little pain-induced fireworks. But the touches were gentle and tingly, period. By the time they reached his lower legs, Joe felt so relaxed he got a fierce hard-on.

He raised his head, eyed the piss-colored tent in the front of his underwear. "That's not about anything," he said.

(I'm in a toilet. The movie was so dull my thoughts kept mutating. It's just some lame, flop, romantic comedy starring what's-his-name and Kathleen Turner. I tried to watch for a half hour, then my eyes naturally flicked to the boy again. His family had settled down. Maybe he'd fallen asleep. All I could see was a sliver of him along the edge of his seat. Sometimes that's plenty. I'm thinking of porn where a guy's body may be exposed but you're still only seeing an aspect of him. You still have to fill in a lot to desire him. For example, I've filled the Dutch boy's big lips with the words, "Kill me, Dennis," among other things. Obscenities. His eyes have grown dull and sleepy, or maybe hyper, or scared, but uncomprehending for sure, like I need eyes to look before I feel comfortable around them. His personality's mechanical and calm, bordering on nonexistent, like a tool. Otherwise he reminds me of every guy I've wanted to fuck and kill. Mostly Pierre at the moment. So Mr. Xerox of Pierre is standing here with his back to the door, looking down at my face, with vague curiosity, I guess. He's naked. I've made him hairless, pale, adolescentlike. My usual. Now I'm at the part in the fantasy that always fucks me over. I want him, specifically his skin, because skin's the only thing that's available. But I've had enough sex in my life with enough guys to recognize how little skin can explain about anyone. So I start getting into this rage about how stingy skin is. I mean, skin's biggest reward, which is sperm, I guess, is only great because it's a message from somewhere inside a great body. But it's totally primitive. Take gold. Would gold be worth anything if there were a more complex, beautiful, similar substance around? I've got a choice. Either I can pretend I'm a psychic or palm reader and tell myself I understand some cute guy if his sperm leaves his body when I'm in his presence, or, as I find myself doing more often these days, I can actually imagine myself inside the skins I admire. I'm pretty sure if I tore some guy open I'd know him as well as anyone could, because I'd have what he consists of right there in my hands, mouth, wherever. Not that I know what I'd do with that stuff. Probably something insane . . . spill the guts through my fingers like pirates supposedly did with doubloons or whatever. Except there'd be a smell, which I guess would be strong and hard to take. I can't imagine it. Maybe the odors of piss, shit, sweat, vomit, and sperm combined. I guess in a perfect world I'd eat and drink all that stuff and not just get nauseous. That's my dream. That's what I'm thinking about. I've got this longstanding urge to really open up someone I'm hot for. The Dutch boy in this case, because he's the latest example. The thought has me sweating and shaking right now. Arms, legs, everywhere. If he were locked in this toilet with me, and if I had a knife, I guess, or claws would be better, I'd shut up that minuscule part of my brain that thinks murder is evil, whatever that means. I'd stand up, or try to stand up, then cut him to pieces. But since I don't have the boy or nerve or weapon, I just sit here scribbling, jerking off. That's what my left hand is doing while this one is writing. But inside my head the most spectacular violence is happening. A boy's exploding, caving in. It looks sort of fake since my only models are splatter films, but it's unbelievably powerful.)

Monday afternoon

A few rows behind Joe a male silhouette sat down next to a poorly lit boy. Joe happened to turn his head, notice. When the house lights dimmed, the mismatched pair sidled into the aisle. He shadowed them past the snack bar, restrooms, up a flight of stairs.

Reaching the landing a few steps ahead of the kid, the man revolved, checked his protégé's progress. "Hey!" The man's eyes veered to Joe, who was ten or so steps behind the kid. "Want something?"

The kid froze mid-step, craned his neck, and looked squarely at Joe too. He seemed twelve, thirteen tops. Ashen, anorexic. A small, battered face like a Halloween mask, with sweet, incongruous eyes.

"Maybe to watch," Joe said, nodding at the kid. "Do *you* mind?"

"*No, I don't,*" the man squeaked in a voice that was obviously supposed to resemble the kid's. He was fiftyish, bald, overweight.

Joe shrugged. "I wouldn't mind, actually."

"Fine." The man waved them up.

The three stumbled onto a hazily lit balcony. It seemed deserted. The kid grabbed a seat on the aisle. Straddling him, crotch to uptilted face, the man hauled his cock out. It wasn't hard. The kid started licking its crusty tip. Joe eased down in the neighboring seat and positioned his face very close to the licks. "Why don't you make him undress?" he wondered aloud, squinting up at the man.

"Because he'd look like shit," the man said. "These kids don't eat anything. They're all junkies. Look." He grabbed a fistful of the kid's brown hair, yanked. "You a junkie?"

"No, ouch," the kid yelped, spitting the cock out. "Don't hurt me."

"You don't shoot?"

"No!" The kid shoved a knuckle between his front teeth and bit down.

"You take dick up your ass?"

"Shometimesh."

The man formed a huddle with Joe and the kid. "You'll french-kiss?" He twisted and yanked the brown hair.

"Ouch! Sure!"

The man winked at Joe. "Any questions?"

Joe was so entertained by this blatant example of cruelty, he had to shake off a touch of hypnosis. "Uh, I'll just watch, like I said."

"Your decision."

The man freed the kid's hair. It stayed sticking up in the air in greasy twists. From Joe's semi-aerial perspective it resembled a little haunted forest. "Wow," he whispered.

"Shit, man. That hurt," the kid mumbled. "I didn't do nothing. Fuck!"

The man nosedove at the kid, open-mouthed. They kissed. That involved so much tonguing and sucking, their faces deflated. Joe could see the exact contours of both skulls. They could have been any two human skulls in the world, more or less.

Bored, Joe turned to the theater's immense, if peripheral movie screen. *A Nightmare on Elm Street* was playing. He'd seen it four, five times. Freddy Krueger, phantom antagonist, lived in the psychotic kingdom of teenagers' dreams. One teen had just woken up bleeding from places where Freddy had stabbed her dream-self. But nobody believed this explanation, not even her boyfriend, an actor who seemed unbelievably familiar from somewhere. "Hmm." Joe spaced out for a few minutes, trying to place him.

Shriek . . . clatter, gurgle . . . shriek . . .

"Wh-wha-what's h-ha-hap-p-pe-pen-ni-ni-ning?" It was the kid. At some point he'd been stripped and folded into a crude ball. His head was wobbling around making heavy-metal-lead-guitarist-style faces. His genitals made Joe think of a plop of dried batter. Occasionally the man's cock would jab at what passed for an ass, not even aiming particularly. Since the hole was the size of a small can of paint, he didn't have to.

"Wh-wha-what's tha-that s-sou-sound?"

"Freddy Krueger just killed the girl's boyfriend," Joe said.

"H-how?"

"He sucked him into the bed and ripped his skin off or something," Joe said. "Then the mattress raised up and exploded like a volcano."

"G-gr-great." The kid smiled, shut his eyes. He looked dead. "I l-lo-love F-Fr-Fre-Fred-d-dy K-Kr-Krue-g-ge-ger."

"Me too," Joe sighed. He felt extremely happy for about three and a half seconds.

* * *

(It turns out that pampered boy really is sick. Our plane just landed in New York and some men had to come with a stretcher and take him off before the rest of us could debark. When they lifted him out of his seat I got a better look at his body. I think he has cancer or AIDS. He's very thin and his eyes have a half-scared, half-dead quality. He's not my type at all. Shit. If I'd seen . . . So I take back that part where I wanted to dismember him and all that. It never happened.)

Monday afternoon

The library's domed lobby towered up, off-white and cracked in spots like a huge egg or skull. Shafts of light poured from its rusty-edged windows, filling the skull with gigantic dust crosses and X's. Crossing the room, Joe literally had to shake off their weird, fake, impressive effect.

"I want to research the history of my neighborhood," he told a tiny, hunched-over librarian.

She peered up from the book she was reading, frowned. Wrinkles deepened all over her face, especially around the mouth where they made a set of perfect parentheses. "Where do you live?" she asked in a scratchy voice.

"They call it the Oaks."

"Who calls it the Oaks?" She closed the book. It was Steven King's *It*. In the cover art, *I* and *t* were formed out of cartoonish human bones against a corpsy blue background.

"People who don't live there," Joe said.

"I'll tell you what." The librarian extended an arthritic finger. "If you walk through those shelves over there you'll see a door. Knock loudly. An elderly gentleman will answer. Tell him what you've just told me."

Joe's eyes traced the trembling digit down a long, shadowy, book-lined aisle. A card taped to this end of the shelving read CRIME A TO G.

He walked, knocked, asked. An even more ancient man in a

fraying black suit led him into a room packed with file cabinets. The geezer shuffled to one, bent down, fished around in a drawer, and came up with a manila file bloated with newspaper clippings. They'd formed a ragged brown crust on three sides of the folder.

"I don't mean to be personal," the old man wheezed, centering the file on a small desk mid-room, "but . . . *why?* We don't often see younger people, at least not in this part of the library."

"I found a bone in my basement," Joe said, sitting down at the desk. "I'm curious how it got there because it's human, apparently. And I'm twenty-six." He opened the file.

Five-eighths of his way through the material, Joe noticed a bulging envelope. The words "Mysterious murder in Oaks" were handwritten shakily across it. He undid the flap, slid out some clippings, and read a dozen.

One time he rested his eyes on the old man, who'd settled into a chair with a copy of *Life* magazine from the fifties. Maybe because he was so old, each time he stayed still for even one, two seconds, Joe was afraid he had died.

Joe spent about a half hour reading.

On June 13, 1967, a dismembered male had been found in some weeds a few doors down Joe's street. The "mysteriousness" came in four parts. First, there was no apparent motive. Second, parts of the body were still missing. Third, the victim remained unidentified. Fourth, no suspects were in custody. One of the clippings included a sketchy portrait. Its caption read: "Victim—male, Caucasian, approx. 23 to 28 years old, shoulder-length brown hair, 5'10", medium build."

Sounds a little like me, Joe thought vaguely. He snorted, shook his head. "Oh, *great*." He pocketed the clipping.

(I'm outside the baggage claim area. There's a minute or two before the shuttle bus gets here that takes me to one of those car rental agencies. Hertz, I think. I just realized the major reason I'm so nonchalant about death is that no one I knew ever died until the last few years, when I was already pretty removed and amoral. Before then, someone else dying was strictly a sexual fantasy, a plot device in certain movies I liked. When people died in those contexts, the loss or effect or whatever was already laundered before it reached me. It was a loss to a particular storyline, say, but nothing personal. So now that ex-boyfriends have started to die off, the situation is really unique, even incomprehensible. The only thing I can do, friends and journalists tell me, is cry. But the idea of death is so sexy and/or mediated by TV and movies I couldn't cry now if someone paid me to, I don't think. I'm just weirdly, intensely entertained by the thought of a boy being deep in the ground and unreachable. I guess I've been thrown out of whack by actual deaths in some way, in terms of getting work done and maintaining routines. Sometimes I've tried to imagine and upgrade the deaths, making them scarier, messier, quicker. I sprawl in bed, dreaming up a spectacular ending for someone, say Samson (R.I.P.), usually while I'm jerking off, since that's the only time I ever feel anything about anyone else. Then I rerun the new death until its details are so familiar, and the actor in question so dead, that I'm ready to cast, kill, bury someone fresh. Pierre, say.)

Monday night

Joe imagined his back, ass, legs being punched by a freckled fist. That relaxed him a little. Then he reached for the phone and dialed the number he'd scribbled on the back of a Sears sales slip.

"No one's around," announced a phone machine. "Give me something to come home to." *Beep*.

"Hi," Joe said. "I . . . uh, waited on you at Sears the other day? And this guy who I work with named Samuel—I'm not sure how well you know him—said you like to whack guys around in bed. I'm, uh, into that too, so—"

Gary picked up. "Hold on a second," he said. His voice sounded less friendly than the recording's. There was a second beep. "Go on."

"Well, like I said, you supposedly whack—"

"Yeah, maybe. What do you look like?"

"You don't remember?" Joe said. "The other day? Well, I'm supposed to look almost exactly like Keanu Reeves, the actor. Know him? He was the nice kid in *River's Edge*. Also he played the best friend of the guy who killed himself in that film *Permanent Record*. Except I'm kind of battered up. Not my face, though."

Gary's hand covered the phone for a second. That's how it sounded at least. Then . . . "Why would someone who looks like Keanu Reeves want to fuck himself up?" The hand immediately covered the phone again.

Joe scanned his living room. "I don't know." His eyes stopped on the bone.

"Good answer."

Joe didn't care what that meant. He carried the phone across the room to his bookcase. He grabbed the bone off its place on the second shelf down from the top and started studying it. "Can I come see you now?"

"No." Gary's hand covered the phone for a second. "Wait a couple of hours. Eleven, eleven-thirty . . ."

"Mm-hm." Joe shoved the bone under his arm, copied down the address. It was only a few blocks away. He thought about saying so. Gary hung up before he could. Once his hands were free, Joe plucked the newspaper article out of his shirt pocket, laying it and the bone side by side on the rug. "Hmm." Although the victim looked so much like him that the sketch could have been a dirty little mirror, Joe found the guy sort of unsympathetic. As for the bone . . . well, it didn't particularly add or detract anything. Joe's mind drifted away. "Weird." Case solved, he thought.

He laid the clipping and bone on the bookshelf, settled into his armchair, lit a cigarette. A few seconds later he walked back and slipped the clipping under the bone so it wouldn't accidentally blow off.

He turned on the TV, switching around with the remote control unit until something violent appeared. His memory of the portrait and bone immediately blanked as his eyes started noting the action.

Two men were backing a teenager across the roof of a tenement. They accused him of robbery. "Don't," he said. As the three neared the edge, the taller of the two men grabbed the seat of the boy's blue jeans, lifting him off his feet. "Don't!" The man carried the boy for a few yards, threw him over the roof. "Do-o-o—!"

(I'm at the hotel. It took only five or six minutes of phone calls to snag that hustler. He's working for one particular escort service that handles a lot of gay porn stars. Man Age Models. I didn't actually talk to him, but the guy who arranges the trysts set one up for an hour from now. Pierre will be by. He costs $200 for "regular" sex, $250 and up for "rough stuff," which the phone guy described as "whatever you two dudes decide." Great.)

(Later. Pierre's here ten minutes early. He's not really French. I feel totally unprepared. Shit. I told him to take a shower but not get his hair wet. He's in the bathroom right now. I hear splashing. This is just a quick note to say that while he's beautiful and everything, though slightly disappointing in person like everyone always is when you know them from reproduction, I'm suddenly struck by the problem of how to get what I want out of him, whatever that is. He immediately asked what I had in mind, the way hustlers do. I could barely talk I was so on the edge, but I said safe, intense sex. A lie obviously. He said okay kind of warily, maybe because I was being so vague. It is vague for me.)

(Pierre just turned off the shower. He's about to come out. I think I'm ready. It's hard to describe these moments . . .)

Monday night

Joe trailed Gary into a stuffy den. Overfurnished with scratched-up antiques, it had three tiny, sepia-colored windows. He went to a pane, cupped his eyes, peered out. The guy's yard belonged in a children's book. Far, far off, half-obscured by trees, he could see a kind of giant-sized doll house whose windows glowed like kerosene lanterns.

Gary was mixing gin and tonics. "You want a little pain-killer in this?" he yelled. "You won't taste it."

"Nah. I've got this weird nervous system or something that doesn't work right." Joe smiled at the doll house.

"Lucky me." A full glass appeared by Joe's left shoulder, followed by Gary's face. Joe turned, took the former.

Ding.

They carried their glasses outside.

"So, what are some of the movies you've acted in, Gary?" Joe was trailing the actor along a path roofed with the limbs of fruit trees. Oranges, lemons, pears, apples . . . Perched in their branches, brightly colored birds blinked at the passing intruders. The night smelled intensely of punch. Joe smiled, batted some flying bugs.

"Third-rate crap." Gary ducked. "Watch this limb. I doubt you've seen any. *Friday the Thirteenth, Part Six*, maybe?" They'd reached the doll house. "Look familiar? Ever see that old "Twilight Zone" episode where nobody ever grew up? This was the main character's home. Warner Brothers was throwing it out, believe it or not." He inserted a key, turned it. "Two hundred bucks."

The interior was painted black. A large X made of two massive pieces of wood, maybe seven feet long, one wide and deep, stood upright room center, decorated with handcuffs. The floor was an inch deep in whips, paddles, knives, etc. Joe stood in the middle, hands on his hips, peering around, impressed. "Wow."

Gary balanced on one leg, removing a sock. "Thanks. Strip."

Joe undressed, which took a fairly long time because stuff kept getting snagged on his scabs. Gary finished first and leaned back on the X, right hand jerking his cock, left hand pinching a cord that dangled from a light bulb perched up in the rafters. "Oh, by the way," he muttered, fingering the cord. "You don't look anything like Keanu Reeves." He yanked. *Click, click.*

The room grew dark gray. Joe could still detect Gary, the X. "Do you want me against that?" he asked, pointing through Gary's chest.

"Good guess." Gary stepped aside.

Joe walked over, revolved, and made his nude body into an X. Gary reached up, *snap, snap,* bent down, *snap, snap,* securing things. Then he backed off a few feet and stood there, jerking off. After a minute or two, that looked boring, to Joe at least. He cleared his throat. "Ahem," he added.

"I'm making a decision," Gary whispered.

"Can I help?"

"Not really." Gary backed into a shadow. "It's like this," he continued quietly. "I always fantasize murdering people I play with, but something usually stops me. I think it's beauty. But whatever it is, it's not there with you. I really want to kill you. It doesn't seem romantic at all. It feels like the practical thing to do."

"That's interesting," Joe said. "But what exactly are you saying?" It was impossible to tell from the actor's expression.

"What . . . I . . . just . . . said." The phrase left Gary's mouth at a trudge, like it was physically deformed or weighed some incredible amount.

"Well, um, you shouldn't do it, because I don't want you to, and I'm half of this." Joe tried to gesture emphatically.

"If I don't do it," Gary said, "that'll be why. But it's the only reason, which is strange, because there should be others, right?" He crouched down, rummaging through the articles on the floor. *Clink, bang, tinkle* . . .

"But you're not going to do it. That's what I need to hear you say." . . . *Clunk, clang, ding, thump.* Gary held up a knife, smiled. "Answer me, Gary," Joe said, almost yelling.

Gary strolled toward Joe, still smiling, knife shaking wildly in one hand, cock scrunched up in the other. "I really think I'm going to kill you," he said hoarsely. "I can't fucking believe it."

The knife stopped just short of Joe's right nipple. Joe gazed at the nipple. Then he gazed at the point of the knife. He raised his eyes to Gary's tight little smile. He lowered his eyes to the smudge of pre-come on the head of his own cock. When he shut his eyes a second later, the four things—pink nipple, knife point, crinkly smile, white smudge—were superimposed against the reddish darkness of his lids. It looked like a flower. "God, Gary, you know what?" he said. "I—"

Stab.

SPACED

1987–1989

Pierre sits on the edge of the bed, gently kicking a wet towel. It's on the rug where he dropped it. First it looks like a twist of whipped cream. Another kick, it's discarded gift wrapping. Kick, a scroll. I'm perched to his right, elbows balanced on my knees, chin in the heels of my palms, staring down at the scroll or whatever. "Thinking?" Pierre whispers, kicks.

"It's complicated," I say, turning to see him. My eyes zigzag down his chest, stomach, crotch like they're watching a tiny or distant rock climber. "If you mean me," Pierre sighs, "I'm easy. If you mean you, well, what can I do to help?" My eyes have drifted back to the towel, which glows in them. "Usually the problem's simple," he continues. "I'm not what you expected, or maybe you're nervous or shy . . ."

"No." I shake my head. "You're exquisite. I mean, there's this mental transition you have to make—and I'm not saying *you* specifically, I mean the collective 'you' or whatever—

65

when you've experienced someone as an image and suddenly he's sitting here talking to you. You have to reevaluate him, but I've done that. And you're great."

"Mm," Pierre says, glances at his watch, which is all he's wearing apart from a thin, gold bracelet. "But, uh, fourteen minutes are already up." I nod vaguely. "It's not always the case," I add. "Certain people don't translate. Like that pretty brunet in that porn video, *Pleasure Mountain*? Scotty was so 'me.' Ever see it? But when I actually bought him, well . . . maybe he'd just gotten older but . . ."

Pierre lies back on the bed, entwines his fingers, cradles his head with them. "Mm-hm." I turn sideways, stare into his crotch. "Like, kids want to befriend their favorite cartoon characters. I did. Well, my dad took me to Disneyland so I could meet them. He aimed me at these huge walking toys and, well, I tried but . . . they couldn't even alter their facial expressions.

"That Scotty was similar. I mean, he looked vaguely like the star of the video I'd loved, but there was something wrong in his—" Pierre feels a grin sneaking up. "Weird," he says. "Anyway, why don't you suck my cock." He hates spouting clichés like that. Still he checks my expression to see if it's worked. I'm shaking my head. "Or lick my ass," he adds. "Fuck me with a condom, uh . . ."

"Your skin, you mean," I mumble. Pierre raises his head. "What?" I reach down, pinch an inch of his thigh, jiggle it like a faulty house key. "Skin," I repeat. "I get to use your skin, and the little areas of your skeleton I can feel underneath, and whatever I manage to squeeze or suck out." Pierre feels confused, which must look ultra-unappealing. So he relaxes his face.

Then he props himself up on his elbows. "Yeah, uh, okay." "Well . . ." I lean down, sniff his crotch. "That's information. Crotches smell pretty identical from guy to guy, if they're clean." I sniff again. "But because you're a beauty, the smell's more profound. Still, what does it tell me that a hundred other men haven't already learned. No, the profound stuff's in here." I poke his stomach.

Pierre's face gets confused again. Shit. "Go on." He hopes I'm too spaced out to care. "Well, if I think you're one of the most extraordinary boys I've ever seen, and I do, then logging your tastes, smells, sounds, textures isn't enough somehow, for me at least. I want to know *everything* about you. But to really do that, I'd have to kill you, as bizarre as that sounds."

"Maybe." Pierre squints at me. I look calm, but if the slightest insanity distorts my face, voice, he's ready to leap for his clothes. "So that's what I'd do, if I was courageous—kill you. I'll dream I'm killing you while I go over your body. I'll seem like your usual sex fiend, but I'll actually be far away in a place where your life's meaningless and your body's carved open."

Jesus, Pierre thinks. "You know," he says, "I do this a lot, fuck for money. I just came from another guy, in fact. But it's true that the way men deal with me is like I'm a kind of costume that someone else, someone they've known or made up, is wearing. The way they look in my eyes and the way they look at my skin is completely different. Is that what you mean?"

I'm looking intently at his cock, which I've stretched very taut. It looks like a fat, misshapen rubber band. "No." I let it go. It lands, wobbling, on his thigh. "Really, you should just know that you fascinate me so much that in a perfect world I'd kill you to understand the appeal. If there's any way you can take that as a supreme compliment, do."

"I'll try." Pierre glances at his watch. "So, are you planning to pay for a second hour?" he asks. "Because otherwise . . ." I nod, my hand swimming around on his sandy-colored stomach, in the cove between his hipbones and ribs. "For now just lie quietly," I whisper. "Get stoned if you want." "I don't do

drugs," Pierre says, reaching for a pillow. "I need to keep an eye on stuff."

For the next forty, forty-five minutes, Pierre receives the ultimate, detailed massage. That's how it feels. Still, so little of me actually skims him and what does touch down is so wet or pointy, or moves so continuously, that he has to raise his chin five, six times and reorient himself in the hotel. I'm always right there inching gradually up his body, hunched down like I'm licking a very large envelope.

From the thighs down, Pierre's dry if kind of grungy. From crotch to neck, which I'm currently studying, he's varying degrees of soaked, tingling. He's relaxed enough generally to mumble some pointers—what feels good, what's boring— some of which I acknowledge with grunts, snorts, moans. Now I'm licking his left ear. "So what are you thinking?" he asks.

My tongue leaves his ear for a second. "Lots." It relands with a squish. A few minutes later I start breathing normally, lean back. Pierre figures I'm bored, rolls over onto his side. "Phew, I—" "Wait," I say. "I'm almost finished. Uh, could you spit in my mouth?" I cringe hopefully. "Or we could kiss," I add. Pierre stiffens. "I don't kiss." "Fine." "I just can't." "No problem." "My boyfriend . . ."

I lie back, fix my eyes on the ceiling. "Line up your mouth with mine. Then I'll do this." I open my mouth very wide, as though I'm screaming. I shut it. "You cough up as much as you can. Okay?" Pierre poises over me, aims. I really do look like I'm screaming. Whereas his face feels so slack he probably looks retarded. As if I'd notice. Besides my open mouth smells so . . . He sniffs.

He lowers his nose, inhales a bit more of my breath. "That's really weird," he mutters. I close my mouth. "What?" He looks in my eyes, which are tense, pissed, alert, *something*. He doesn't care what I'm feeling one way or another. *Au contraire*. "That I can smell my body in your mouth. I mean, it's happened before with guys, sure, but I've never paid much attention."

I squint. "Really?" "Yeah. Look, reopen your mouth." I do. Pierre bends, sniffs. "I definitely smell sweat, B.O., whatever." Sniff. "My ass. And there's something else too, but it's vague." He peeks at me, snickers. "This is fun. Weird, but fun. Okay, get ready." He starts coughing and snorting up stuff from the darker recesses of his throat and nose.

He emits grayish goo in a long, unbroken, lumpy thread. Then he wipes his lips. I swallow noisily. "Thanks. The only other thing is"—I prop myself up on my elbow— "when I was fingering your ass, I felt some shit. So could you use the toilet and not flush it? And piss into one of those glasses?" Pierre has to bunch up his lips to keep from laughing.

"I'm not being abject," I say. "It's not, 'Ooh, shit, piss, how wicked,' or anything. It's, like I said, information." Pierre nods. "Then what are you going to do with it?" he asks. "I don't mean with my shit, I mean with the information." My face scrunches up. "Uh, create a mental world . . . uh, wait. Or a situation where I could kill you and understand . . . Shit, I sound ridiculous."

Pierre shrugs. "Well, you do and you don't." My eyes fix on the sheet that separates me from him. They startle or widen, like they're seeing something miraculous. "It's really hard to articulate this," I say. "I didn't used to try, because it was a mindless urge. But ever since I started to analyze it, it's gotten so complex and clouded with daydreams, theories . . .

"Like those fringe cults who believe UFOs founded the earth? Obviously there could be zillions of species out there in the universe. I'm sure UFO cultists used to be curious, period, like anyone else, but now they've thought . . . too hard? Their thoughts are over-elaborate and impractical. They can't think, well, three-dimensionally. Maybe I'm like them in a certain way, but I'm much more pragmatic.

"I mean, I know there's no God. People are only their

bodies, and sex is the ultimate intimacy, etc., but it's not enough. Like you. I find what I know about you amazing, *so* amazing I can't get beyond my awe. So part of me wants to dismantle that awe or whatever, and see how you work. But I know that's selfish. Your life's as important as anyone's, including mine . . . so, I'm stuck.

"Maybe . . . if I hadn't seen this . . . snuff. Photographs. Back when I was a kid. I thought the boy in them was actually dead for years, and by the time I found out they were posed photographs, it was too late. I already wanted to live in a world where some boy I didn't personally know could be killed and his corpse made available to the public, or to me anyway. I felt so . . . enlightened?

"Or maybe it wasn't feeling at all, but shock or numbness or . . . I don't know. I think of it as religious. Like insane people say they've seen God. I saw God in those pictures, and when I imagine dissecting you, say, I begin to feel that way again. It's physical, mental, emotional. But I'm sure this sounds psychotic and . . . oh, blah, blah, blah, blah."

Pierre shrugs. "It's sort of sad," he says. I take a breath, let it out. "Probably." He eases off the bed, spends a half minute stretching, fingers to toes, swiveling side to side. "It was kind of pointless to explain myself," I announce, smiling badly. "Still, better you than my journal, I guess. And you really are beautiful, but I've said that a hundred times." Pierre shrugs. "Thanks."

He pulls the bathroom door shut, feeling stiff and hard to operate. He hadn't noticed how stiff until now. Plus, he looks pinker, shinier than usual. "And sticky." He walks to the toilet, arms straight out like Frankenstein. Then he unwraps a glass, fills it with piss, which is orangy from all the vitamin B's he gulps. Then he squirts the extra piss into the sink, turns on cold.

He sits on the toilet, pushes a turd out, stands, yanks a handful of TP and wipes himself. The turd floats in the blue water, reeking. Pierre tries to inhabit the thoughts of someone who'd think shit is a message from someone who laid it, but he's too fucking normal and too deeply into hustler-robot mode. He wonders if I want the TP kept separate, then thinks, Who cares, drops it into the bowl.

Pierre wakes up for good. As he's lying there yawning, he vaguely remembers a couple of false starts inspired by a ringing phone. He looks to his left. It's eleven. Next thing, he's stumbling down the hall toward his phone machine. "Wait. Coffee," he whispers in a shredded voice, veering into the kitchen. He does what he has to, then plays back the messages, sips.

Beep. "It's Paul at Man Age. Appointment, twelve-thirty P.M., hour, Gramercy Park Hotel, room three-forty-four, name Terrence. Later." *Beep*. "Paul again. Appointment, two P.M., Washington Annex Hotel, room six-twenty, a play-it-by-ear, name Dennis, I think the same Dennis from last night. Check with us mid-afternoon. You're a popular dude. Later." *Beep*. "P., it's Marv, you there? . . . No? . . . Call me at work. Love ya."

On his way to the shower Pierre makes a stop at the stereo, plays side one of *Here Comes the Warm Jets*, an old Eno album. It's still on his turntable. It has this cool, deconstructive, self-conscious pop sound typical of the '70s Art Rock Pierre loves. He doesn't know why it's fantastic exactly. If he were articulate, and not just nosy, he'd write an essay about it.

Instead he stomps around in the shower yelling the twisted lyrics. " 'By this time/I'd got to looking for a kind of/substitute . . . ' " It's weird to get lost in something so calculatedly chaotic. It's retro, pre-punk, bourgeois, meaningless, etc. " '. . . I can't tell you quite how/except that it rhymes with/dissolute.' " Pierre covers his ears, beams, snorts wildly.

Tying his sneakers, he flips the scuffed-up LP, plays his two

favorite songs on the second side, which happen to sit third
and fourth, and are aurally welded together by some distorted
synthesizer-esque percussion, maybe ten, fifteen seconds in
length. Pierre flops back in his chair, soaks the interlude up. It
screeches, whines, bleeps like an orgasming robot.

All the way to the hotel, that sound rattles around in his
head, gradually fragmenting into the sound of the cab's mo-
tor. The lobby's faint Muzak is gruesome—old Beatles,
homely as a buzzing mosquito. It follows him into the eleva-
tor, down the third-floor hall. 338, 340, 342 . . . He knocks.
The door's thrown back by a nude, dyed-blond, pockmarked
troll.

"Hi, Pierre. I'm Terrence," the troll says. He revolves and
walks into the room. He has one of those bodies that's thin-
nish at the top, fat bottomed and ripply on the sides, sort of
like a jug. "I love your videos," he continues, sitting down on
the bed, crossing his hairy legs. "But they don't show your
armpits enough. Your pits are spectacular, you know, and
vastly, vastly underrated."

Pierre just stands there. He has slid his hands into his back
pockets. That's supposed to signify boredom, cockiness—
qualities that troll-types admire. Whatever works. "So, undress from the waist up and lie down," Terrence says. "But
first, do you use a deodorant?" Pierre nods. "Well, I may ask
you to wash it out. We'll see." "You said pants *on*, right?"
Pierre mutters, yanking his shirttails out.

Faceup on the bed, fingers entwined behind his head, Pierre
waits patiently while Terrence sniffs first one armpit, then the
other. The troll's on his hands and knees, back so pockmarked
it looks like a turtle shell. "They're perfect," he moans. "Purr
. . . fect." His voice turns to breath. "Hurmph." Something
like that. He starts guzzling a pit—tongue, teeth, lips blended
together.

The view keeps reminding Pierre of different stuff. Sometimes the armpit hairs stand in a skinny brown stalk, with

Terrence's lips as its flower. Then the hairs will come to a point and twist slightly at the tip like chocolate ice cream or smoke. They spread out to resemble a big, dirty dandelion. The troll mashes them down, they're wheat pasta steaming in a white bowl.

When Terrence switches over to pit #2, his double chin blocks the view. So Pierre watches the last few standing hairs in the abandoned pit droop into a swampy pile. Then he slides one hand loose, focuses on his watch, and counts down the rest of the hour, rerunning some particularly nonsensical Eno lyrics in his head. With three minutes to go, the troll comes, says, "You're . . . *great.*"

There's enough time to walk to the Washington Annex Hotel, so Pierre strolls across Seventeenth Street, left at Park Avenue, across the park, down University Place. It's late enough in the fall that people's tans are just yellowish shells cracked and peeling in spots to show the real, milky guys underneath. Pierre's into guys whose coloring keeps them indoors a lot. That's Marv's biggest selling point.

Thought of Marv's naked white body twisted for sex reminds Pierre of saliva, which makes him picture his own dribbling into my mouth. He's climbing the spiral staircase to my hotel room, half backing out of the meeting, mentally anyway. It's the shit-piss agenda. It's not that he minds sharing those things with strangers. It's just . . .

On the one hand, they're trash. They should cease to exist as soon as they leave Pierre's hips. Even cavemen knew that, he thinks. Shit, piss are presents for dogs out on walks at best. If they have any message, it's got to be very disguised and intricate, since it takes guys with eight years of med school to send word some shitter or pisser is sick.

"Oh, fuck it." Pierre knocks. He's a few minutes early, which explains the delay in my answering, as well as some banging around in the meantime, right? When I open up, disheveled, smiling, he remembers how harmless I seemed in relation to what I was spouting, like those angelic singers in satanic rock bands, but less cute. I lead him in, sit on the bed, pat a spot to my right.

"I thought," I say, "maybe we'd just talk this time, since I've gotten you figured out, physically anyway." I blink at him. He sits on the bed. "Okay, sure." ". . . Because it was fascinating to say all that stuff to you, stuff I usually just write in my journal, and you didn't seem to mind." "No, it's fine." ". . . And it could help me to get my ideas in the open." Pierre shrugs. "You got it."

"So . . ." I stand up abruptly, go over and lean on the wall by the fake-wood desk/dresser. ". . . uh . . ." I twist my lip, eyes following an invisible fly. Pierre has relaxed and is fingering one of his brown curls. When he's not on the job, his shoulders tend to slump forward. This time he lets them slump. "Well," he mumbles, "you were talking last time about how you'd kill me if . . . well, I forget why."

"Right, yeah." My eyes steady and pin Pierre. "Like I flew out here from Los Angeles thinking I'd kill you. That was the fantasy. Obviously, I didn't make any provisions for getting away with it, so I guess it was never a real goal, but I took all these notes on the way about wanting to do it." I point at my open suitcase. There are papers, heavily marked, scattered over the contents.

"I think," I continue, "No, I *know* that if I killed you, and it wouldn't have to be *you*, just someone who, like you, fits a particular physical type that I'm into, it would be unbelievably profound. I'd be . . . free? That sounds stupid, I guess. But I see these criminals on the news who've killed someone methodically, and they're free. They know something amazing. You can just tell.

"And I want to know that . . . thing. I've wanted to know it since I was thirteen and . . . blah, blah, blah." Pierre looks vacantly down his chest, through the slot of his shirt collar. There are six or seven lightning-bolt hairs on his chest that he

shaves before video shoots. Sometimes they accidentally seem
to form letters or Roman numerals. XII at the moment.
"Yeah?" he says, hearing I've paused.

"Can you relate to any of this?" I'm frowning at him. Pierre
shrugs. "Only the weirdness," he says. "I appreciate things
that could be considered a little off." "Like what?" Pierre
smiles down at his deflated nipples, creased stomach. "Music," he says. "Seventies Art Rock. Eno, Roxy, Sparks, T.
Rex? Know that period?" I seem to nod. "Well," he adds,
"that's a pathetic comparison, but . . ."

My face is adrift again. Well, mainly the eyes and especially
my mouth, which hangs partway open. It's pink and kind of
too dry inside. It looks a little bit like a doll chair, at least from
ten feet away. There's something generally pleasant about my
face, Pierre decides. That should make my insanity eerier.
Maybe he's being too nonchalant. Or maybe I'm totally harmless, just . . . Who knows?

"I feel like I'm boring you," I say. Pierre shrugs. "Boredom
isn't an issue, and anyway, you're not." I sort of fidget, sniff.
"Well, I'm glad." Pierre flops back, wriggling across the bed
until he can reach a pillow, which he slides under his head.
The cool cotton reminds him of something. He tries to home
in on the memory. It involves Marv. "Why don't you . . . ?

". . . Why don't you make what you're saying a story?"
Pierre says. He raises up, squints at me. "Like if I was a kid,
and you were trying to help me get sleepy and teach me
something new at the same time. Sometimes my boyfriend
does that, tells me weird stories based on his day at work.
Maybe that way I'd understand better, or . . . But I mean, it's
your hour." I nod hurriedly. "Okay, let me think."

"Well, a friend of mine, Samuel, was in love with a young
guy he worked with, okay? Samuel used to obsess about Joe,
who apparently was very 'me.' Tall, pale, dark hair, thin,

boyish, spaced-out. Like you. So I kept saying, 'If you ever get over him, introduce me.' In the meantime, whenever Samuel and I hung around, I'd asks tons of questions about Joe, being obsessive myself.

"Samuel found it hard to approach Joe, because the guy was so spaced-out or private or both. Lots of staring off into the air, vague answers, which struck Samuel as very Mona Lisa–esque. He'd follow Joe around the store studying his manner, waiting for the perfect moment to ask him to dinner or something. That took weeks. Samuel was just getting shyer and more confused.

"One night on the phone we added up what Samuel knew about Joe. I had paper and pen at my end, making a list. We decided that Joe was probably just as obsessive as Samuel, only not about sex and love, but about splatter films, which was mostly what Joe talked about when he talked. I like them too, not surprisingly, I guess, which made me even more curious about Joe.

"Samuel's not into violence at all. He's very romantic, despite his cynicism. So I gave him some tips, buzz words, splatter codes, to try out on Joe, in terms of getting to know the guy. Of course I was hoping Samuel would lose interest, but not before getting to know Joe well enough to play Cupid for us. Because the guy sounded perfect, and I was still boyfriend-oriented at that point. This was a year ago.

"Apparently it got so Joe and Samuel would have weird little talks during lulls at work, with my friend asking questions and Joe half responding, half daydreaming. Still, Joe was easily distracted, and if Samuel could keep up one straight line of thought for a while, especially on the subject of violence, Joe would follow it. That was enough for a couple of months.

"Let's see. I forget how it happened, but thanks partially to my urgings, Samuel got around to the subject of sex. Essentially he asked Joe to sleep with him, pretty much straight out. I think Joe's reaction was on the order of, 'That's weird,' something very ambiguous. Hope for us both. Samuel brought it up several times over two, three weeks. Joe shrugged, yawned, etc.

"One day Samuel was lucky or something. Joe said, 'Sure, why not?' So ... This is wild. They went back to Samuel's place, and it turns out that Joe, who, like I said, is supposedly my ultimate physical type, is a masochist. He's covered with scars, cuts, welts, stuff like that from his earlier encounters. And Samuel, *the wimp*, freezes up, spanks him a few times.

"Next day he calls me, recounts the scene. Obviously I flip. Samuel mopes a bit, then agrees reluctantly to introduce me to Joe sometime the next week. I mean, you can imagine, based on what little you know about me, how it stank of fate or whatever. This guy who wants to die, even if that just means dying metaphorically, and me, impotent murderer ...

"I spent most of the weekend with Samuel pumping him for every shred of Joe info. Physical details, habits, opinions the guy had let slip about music or TV he liked, background stuff. I still have an unfinished novel I tried to write based on all this. Anyway, I was wandering around dazed and horny or psychotic or whatever it is that comes over me, waiting for 'next week.'

"Well, Joe never showed up for work. Not for months. Eventually it turned out this actor whose name I forget— you'd know his face—murdered Joe during some violent S&M scene. They dug Joe's dismembered corpse out of the actor's backyard. I felt really conflicted about it. I mean, *I* could have killed him, or not killed him, but known him, explored stuff with him.

"Because I don't want to kill anyone, not really, not if it means being selfish, which murderers basically are. But here was this guy who might have shared these obsessions. Shit. It's like my whole fucking life has been a series of near-misses, in terms of people. I let my first boyfriend, Julian—this weird, amoral explorer of bodies like me but more clever—I let him drift off.

"And Julian's kid brother, Kevin, who I got involved with later. He seemed insane at the time, but I think he was something like Joe, only at an earlier stage of development. Really passive, spaced-out, always accidentally hurting himself, very puttylike. So cute, and all bruised ... The thought of him drives me wild now, but at the time he seemed like too big a responsibility.

"The only guy I ever actually got violent with was a hardcore punk type in the days when I hung around those kinds of scenes. Samson, a fake name, I'm sure. He's dead now. Of AIDS. I beat him up, to see what it felt like. I thought I'd killed him for a while. Anyway, I just remember it as a weird, fluky experience. It doesn't seem to have anything to do with my obsession, though it obviously must.

"I don't know why it doesn't, except the scene was so unsophisticated, unlike my mental image of violence, which is more like a film. I'm sure I've idealized brutality, murder, dismemberment, etc. But even slicked up, there's an unknowableness there that's so profound or whatever, especially when I combine it with sex. Then it's—I'm—out of control. Inside.

"It's incommunicable, obviously. Listen to me. I should either do it, or not do it and see a psychiatrist or whatever. Because it's infecting everything for me now. I flew here daydreaming of killing you, without a specific plan, not having told anyone I know. It's stupid, pointless. And I'm repeating myself, so ... Maybe you should just go. Here ... here's your two hundred dollars." I dig around for my wallet.

Six months later, Pierre refolds my newest letter, jabs it into his back pocket. Then he slides off his jeans, settles down on a wicker chair. "Don't sit there!" Warren yells, glaring across the equipment-strewn room. "Use ... your ... head!" Pierre shoots to his feet, twists, looks down his back. The wicker's design is printed perfectly on the buttocks in pink. "Tim," Warren sighs, "massage that crap out."

Pierre folds his arms while the kneeling Tim squishes his ass around. One time he looks back and reads the guy's ruddy face. It seems distant, uninterested, as if Tim were petting a dog or whatever. Still, it feels like the guy cares in some fashion. Clients have stroked him in similarly vague ways when what they actually desire is . . . who knows? Unsafe sex, Pierre guesses.

His costars, two blond guys—one pale, skinny, and big-nosed, the other hefty, tan, hairy-chested—are sitting across a double bed from each other. The latter, Heiner, smooths down his calf hairs, which are so dense his legs appear permanently filthy. Cuter Bob stares at his reflection in a round mirror hanging to the left of the window, overcast with little clouds of cocaine.

"Tim?" It's Warren's voice. "Yeah, yeah," Tim yells. He slaps Pierre's ass. "It's itself again." Pierre checks, nods approvingly, wanders in the direction of Heiner and Bob. Their hazel eyes focus on his. They slide maybe two, three feet farther apart. The bed looks sort of beachy, with blue sheets and green blankets bunched up at one end like the fringe of the Atlantic Ocean.

Pierre wedges himself between the blonds, squints at the camera half-buried in glare, waits. The crew's discussing the lighting, which is apparently too undramatic for Warren. As a director, he's trying to upgrade gay porn with artsy technical details, although the sex is your standard, post-AIDS, "safe" sleaze barely interrupted by thin, sub-sitcom-style narratives. "So where were we?" he mumbles.

The blonds look stupidly at Pierre. "Uh, right," Pierre answers. "Heiner and I have gotten Bob drunk and driven him back to this place, *our* place, I guess, right? To . . . well, *you* tell me." Warren's nodding. "Yeah, right. Bob, you're the centerpiece. Act inebriated for a minute or two, then just get into the sex. Heiner, Pierre, don't forget, the kid drives you berserk."

Pierre shuts his eyes, fondles his cock. Heiner, who masturbates with a huge sawing motion, starts jabbing Pierre in the ribs with his elbow. So Pierre inches closer to Bob, who can harden without any help from his hands. And stay hard. That's why he's ubiquitous in porn at the moment. Great skin too, Pierre thinks, brushing against a relatively hairless stretch.

It usually takes Marv to get Pierre hard. That's why he doesn't get cast very often or very imaginatively, despite his cute, sleepy looks. A year ago he was the boy with the ass every costar was destined to eat, finger, spank, fuck, etc. That way he didn't need to get hard more than thirty, thirty-five seconds per project, footage of which would be chopped up, intercut through the video-at-large.

Now his asshole is overexposed, supposedly. So he has gone from star fuckee to second- or third-string fucker whose occasional lack of a hard-on is evident only to the porn aficionado. Or to hard-core Pierre fans, of which there are obviously a few . . . psychotics . . . He pictures a page of my letter. His hard-on immediately softens. Shit. "Pierre!" Warren yells from somewhere in the glare. "Concentrate!"

Pierre peeks at Bob who has a luxurious look in his eyes that makes his nose seem less big. Heiner's eyes, on the other hand, are a little too narrow and tense, as if they've been condemned to feel whatever they're feeling. "Okay, boys, start doing something fantastic," Warren yells. "Pierre, try your best. Bob, remember you're drunk. Ack—" Pierre cups his limp cock. "—shun!"

Pierre gets it hard on and off for the next hour. When it's not hard, he drops his jaw, squints, groans, and the cameraman shoots his body from the pubes up. "Not a problem, keep going!" Warren shouts to him over and over. After the shoot, everyone but Pierre gets extremely coked up. One by one they file out. As Pierre's leaving, Warren grabs his left biceps. "You, wait."

The way Warren cocks his head, smiles, winks, Pierre guesses he was beautiful in his younger days. Or seductive at least. Even if now, on such an awful physique, that kind of confidence translates as sliminess. "I'll pay you to stick around," Warren says. "Get it up, don't, I could give a shit. I'm into . . ." He draws a girlish butt in the air in front of his face, sticks his tongue out.

Pierre shrugs, stands up, stepping out of his jeans, underwear. "Then I'd better clean up," he says. "One sec." He walks into the bathroom nook, yanks off a few feet of TP, and scrunches it into a flowery wad. He sticks the wad under the tap for a second, dabbing his asshole. He thinks he looks pooped, in the mirror at least. Good thing asses don't communicate their owners' emotional states.

He centers his ass in the mirror, grabs and jerks it around until the flesh empurples, puffs out through his fingers, etc. When he lets go, it's still a smooth, two-part, rectangular slab that must be pretty top-notch as asses go, because enough guys like Warren fixate on it, even if they're just projecting stuff onto it/him, or casting it/him in mental porn movies.

When Pierre reenters the set, Warren's sprawled on the bed reading a short stack of papers, apparently my unfolded letter. The guy must have gone through Pierre's pants. Pierre feels totally stricken, but before he can blurt out some sort of admonishment, Warren looks up, dazed. "Is this real?" he asks, waving the papers. "This guy's . . ." He starts reading again. ". . . out there. *Way* out."

"Yeah, I think so," Pierre says. He walks partway into the room and stands around hugging himself. "Gee, you don't seem like you'd know anybody this nutsy," Warren mumbles. Pierre shrugs. "The guy started writing to me," he says, "about this torture-and-murder-boys fantasy, I guess because

I let him go on about that kind of stuff during sex. I always get weird johns. He was unusually weird though."

Warren puts down the letter. It folds up by itself. "You fucked this guy?" "Sort of," Pierre says. "The sex was extensive, but actually, nothing much happened. He looked at me, licked me a little, and talked a lot." Warren's shaking his head. "Yeah, but *come on*. This guy's a fucking murderer." "Well, if he is," Pierre says, "he was supposedly daydreaming then.

"His thing was he wanted to kill, but he couldn't. I can't remember why not. So he was tortured. He seemed like he knew the limitations. He talked about them with a lot of complexity, like where he thought sexual fantasies came from, tracing his back to incidents in his childhood. I never felt endangered, actually. And now it just seems like a scene in a documentary.

"But, okay, since he moved overseas I think something cracked and he decided to do it because, yeah, I mean *you* read the letter. It sounds like he's actually killing those boys, right? He's not saying, 'I'm transcribing this daydream I had.'" Warren has picked up the letter again. He's squinting down at it, wagging his head. "It sounds real," he says. "But then how would *I* know?"

Pierre flops in a chair. "I don't know what I should do," he says, fingering his hair. "I could write back and say, 'Leave me alone.' Still, I have to admit that I'm kind of addicted to the letters now. But then I'm such a fucking aesthete about everything." "Mm-hm," Warren nods wildly. "If I were you, I'd let him write. That way you can keep a close watch on him. I mean, who knows, I mean . . ."

Warren's eyes get a glary sheen that might or might not be imploding emotion. Strange. Anyway, they're not green anymore. More, well, metallic-hued, like those contacts Peter Gabriel wore to look mechanical when he was in Genesis. Come, lube, sweat decorate the bed sheets with grayish polka dots. Under the lights, they must have started to cook because the area smells like a toasted cheese sandwich.

"I knew a guy," Warren continues. "Possibly equally nuts. To make these porns, see, I have to raise money. And one time I was introduced to this rich old gay guy who was interested in financing porn. I spent some weekends at his place. He wanted to pay me to make a snuff video, a *real* one. He had this cute Asian kid who lived with him who was supposed to be the victim.

"The guy says he'll finance my porns for the rest of my life if I do him this favor and shoot this snuff thing with this Asian kid, him, and a couple of guys I never met who'd do the actual killing. I said no, obviously. No way, of course. But the guy wound up making one anyway, I don't know how. But I know that for sure because, well . . ." Warren falls back in the scrambled sheets.

"A friend of mine in the industry was passed a copy. He described it to me one night, and I thought, Shit. I had him show me the first couple of minutes, before anything really violent happens, and it's that same Asian kid being tied to a bed, looking very, very upset. I said, 'Turn it off.' But part of me thinks, as weird as this sounds, that I blew it.

"I mean, I couldn't even watch the video, so I don't know what I'm imagining, but you know, to have seen that Asian kid being killed in person, if it was going to happen anyway. I mean . . . what an unbelievable thing to experience. After that, you'd never be the same person again, I'm positive. Imagine it. Jesus. But that's easy to say now when there's no fucking way."

Pierre's toying with one of his brown curls. "You sound like that Dennis guy," he says. "Or like Dennis's kid brother. Dennis was more, well, not solemn exactly, but centered about it or something. Hmm . . ." The sky's clouding up outside the window. Either that or it's late and the sunset's unusually colorless. "Nice." He hears Warren's clothes open. A dull, irregular *pop, pop, pop . . .*

The yellow wallpaper's fake-elegant in a vaguely uninterest-ing way. Pierre spaces out studying it. The longer he stares, the more it resembles piss. Yawn. "Get your butt over here," Warren snarls jokingly. He's positioned on the bed, nude, overweight, penis stubby and hard. His hands form what looks like a very small chair. It's poised about a foot or so over his mouth.

As Pierre starts to sit, the chair rises to catch, stop him. "Wait," Warren says. "Have you been tested?" "Yeah, nega-tive." "How's that possible?" Warren mutters. The chair re-configures and grows slightly wobbly. "I don't know," Pierre says. The chair's about to collapse any second. "Well, okay, I believe you." Pierre's ass drops suddenly onto a face that makes a noise like a whoopie cushion.

Nine months later Marv opens the apartment door waving a sealed envelope. Pierre squints, reads the return address. "Shit." He staggers past Marv, drops the grocery bag on the dining room table, and heads down the hall. "Can I open it?" Marv yells after him. "Yeah," Pierre says, then rethinks. "Actually, don't, please? Just wait a . . ." He slams the bedroom door.

The room smells like him, thanks to dirty clothes. Piles. Sometimes he lets himself fantasize bottling that stink or put-ting it in an aerosol can or whatever. It would be sold with a videotape of him jerking off, finger fucking himself, etc. But tonight the smell's painfully reminiscent of something. What? He lands, sniffling, bouncing, on the unmade bed.

Marv knocks. "P.?" "Just wait, okay?" Pierre shouts. "Start dinner, watch TV, whatever. I'll be out in a minute." After ten, fifteen seconds he hears the TV switch on in the living room. News. Plane crash. Tons dead. When he's sure the volume's loud enough, the news sufficiently bad to distract Marv, he starts sobbing. His whole body jerks, jerks, jerks.

The man who'd paid to fuck him this evening was obviously

sick, AIDS, but Pierre had agreed to play saint just so long as the man used a condom, which was probably safe. Still, the guy's eyes were so far away the whole hour, or each time Pierre thought to check, like it either meant nothing or everything to have total access to a sterling, unjudgmental face and ass.

He himself had felt . . . what? Maybe little to zero, as usual. Nevertheless, the guy's fear or pain or whatever rubbed off, as they say. Or it made his own numbness depressing, baffling. When you think about being in bed with somebody, Pierre thinks, sick or not, you're either so far away you think in total clichés, or else you're so close things blur, or . . . Fuck.

"Fuck off." He lies there and shakes, drips, squeaks. Occasionally he holds his breath, makes sure the TV's still on in the other room. After a while he reaches over, picks up the remote control unit, and turns on the TV in this room, leaving the volume down. News. An old picture of what's-her-name rimmed in a thin, black frame, which must mean she's finally dead.

Marv's probably out in the living room, totally upset, not that he cares all that much about what's-her-name. He's just more connected to life's . . . whatever, ups, downs, whereas Pierre feels so little about anything, much less what's-her-name's predictable death. He's too . . . whatever, bored, hardened, worried to have an opinion one way or another.

"P.!" Marv's at the door. "What's-her-name's dead!" "Yeah, I know," Pierre says, cringing at how weak his fucking voice sounds. There's an intense little silence outside the door. "You . . . okay?" Marv asks. The knob turns very slowly. Shit. Pierre throws an arm over his eyes as the light from the hall slants in. Next thing he knows a hand's stroking his curly hair.

"What's up?" Marv whispers. The mattress squeaks and drops a foot near Pierre's shoulder. He can smell Marv, meaning Levi's. Actually it's Tide detergent he smells, not dyed cotton. Still, he associates the smell with his lover for some reason. "Today. The client," Pierre says. "AIDS. It was obvious. And it's weirding me out." He raises the arm as proof.

Marv looks astonished by all the moisture under there. On TV, a drug bust. Rows of boxes of cocaine about to be burned. The idea makes Pierre tingle slightly. "You're cold," Marv whispers. He's eyeing Pierre's raised arm. "Maybe you're ill, like the flu," he adds, running a fingertip over the greenish-white goosebumps. "No," Pierre barks, pulls away.

They sit, lie around there a few endless minutes. Marv gets up, walks through the room like he's hunting for something. The third time he passes the TV set, he spins the volume up, sits on the end of the bed. A father and son are hugging, blubbering, in a circle of cameras and microphones, after the youngster supposedly escaped from a kiddie porn ring.

"You know," Pierre says. "I was about that kid's age when I made . . . well, I think they're calling it *Summer Camp* now, but it was a super-eight loop at the time. I thought the man wanted sex, period, which was scary enough. Then, suddenly, there's this other man holding a camera . . . Now I'm glad it's on record. I look *so* alive in it, *so sharp*. The way that man's gobbling my ass and I'm just going, 'Huh?' "

"Bullshit," Marv says quietly. "You looked terrified. And so does this kid. Watch." He leans forward, turns up the TV even louder. ". . . so my dad," the kid's mumbling, "wouldn't give up on me." "And I won't!" shouts the dad. The kid rolls his eyes in embarrassment. Reporters guffaw. The kid blows a little kiss to the assembled. The dad smacks the kid's head. "God," Marv groans, hurriedly turns down the volume.

"Terrified?" Pierre sniffs, and kicks Marv, not hard enough to hurt. Marv leans way, way forward, spaces out on the screen, or pretends to. A Hyundai commercial. Pierre turns on his side, spaces out on the wall, a little haunted by *Summer Camp*, specifically by the thought of his skinny legs waving around in the air on either side of a man's bald head like antennae.

"But it's weird, Marv," he whispers, "I mean in that *Summer Camp* thing, how amazed I look." Marv doesn't flinch. "If anything from my childhood influenced my adulthood," he continues, "it was that afternoon. To have an older man so completely, insanely worked up over me, like if I was where someone had buried some sort of treasure or antidote to something malignant in him.

"Because, you know, it's supposed to be people succeed in life depending on how many skills they have or lack. But in that loop, what's so great about me has shit to do with any skill. My behavior and ideas and so on are in the way, if anything. Which is insane, right? So what *did* that man see in me? I sure don't see anything great about my stupid little creepy self."

The bed jiggles. Pierre rolls over, squints. Marv's on his feet again. "We've discussed this before," he says. "And I don't know what you're going on about. I'm gonna adjust the temperature of the oven." He splits, slams the door. Typical. Pierre rolls over onto his other side, watches the curtains billow up and deflate around an overcast sky X'ed with telephone wires. He tries to sob, can't.

Eventually he gets up, traipses down the hall. Marv's sitting at the kitchen table reading my letter. Pierre takes some cranberry juice from the fridge, sits down opposite. The stove reeks of broiling chicken. That blends curiously with the taste of the juice. He sips, sniffs, sips, sniffs in quick succession a few times. The combination's, uh, Middle Eastern in some vague way. Oh, so what?

Marv's reading the letter, eyes bugging, brows arched, forehead crumpled. "Any new developments out Amsterdam way?" Pierre asks. Marv shakes his head. "Same old apocalyptic porno. Maybe a little more detailed. The part I'm on now, the victim's real young. Here." He holds it out. "No." Pierre slugs some juice. "I'm so over that sex-and-death stuff. When you're through with it, toss."

Pierre tips his chair back, sips. Marv reads on. His face does its pseudo-shocked vaudeville act. That's the problem, Pierre thinks. You can get used to anything. Then you stop feeling, you just respond, your brain reduces the world to ... whatever ... comedy? He sniffs. Hmm. What's burning? "Marv, what's ... ?" His lover tosses my letter down, flies at the stove with his hand out.

NUMB

1989

Dear Julian,

Maybe you remember. In the early to mid-'70s we used to fuck and hang out for a few years, then you moved to Paris. Years later I ran into you at a club called The Open Grave in New York when I'd renamed myself Spit. We wound up fucking in your hotel. For the record, my first name is Dennis again. Spit was a really brief thing. He existed for maybe a year at most. I'm writing because I suspect you're the one human being I've ever known who'll understand what I'm trying to say, since I feel like I learned virtually everything when we were lovers. I know I seemed weird in that Spit phase, sorry. I'm writing in part to let you know how important you were and still are to me. I should have said so that night, but as you could tell by the pseudonym, I wasn't into connecting with people. I cut off everybody I loved or who

89

loved me. I had to. I'm not sorry I did. I think you'll probably understand why if you just keep reading.

As you can tell by the stamp on the envelope, I live in Holland, Amsterdam to be exact. I originally came over here, meaning Europe, to find you. I spent a couple of weeks down in Paris. My address for you was two or three years out of date, but I eventually located your boyfriend who said you were vacationing in Morocco or something. I trained up to Amsterdam planning to kill time until you got back, but I ended up finding a place.

Anyway, the point is I'm writing to the Julian I imagine you to be. That's a guy who'll relate to the strange, ecstatic situation I'm in. Mainly I'm going to tell you some things because I'll flip if I don't. And I'm going to tell you my story chronologically, to keep myself clear. See how this sounds.

Okay, a year and a half ago I met someone in a coffee shop here where they sell marijuana and hash. They're both legal in Holland, as you probably know. He said he knew a place where I could live for a while. I felt so carefree or insane at that point I thought, Sure, why not live abroad. You'd done it. So this guy guided me to a man who was trying to rent out two floors in a windmill. Problem was the ground floor housed a small brewery, so the upper floors smelled like beer all the time. It's huge and incredibly cheap. Still, the smell's unbelievable, especially during the summer. All I own is a futon, a clock, and some cooking utensils. There's a stove, refrigerator. The floors are two large round rooms stacked on top of each other with a spiral staircase in the center and little porthole-shaped windows. The brewery keeps the rest of the building warm. My mom sends me cash every month via American Express, out of guilt for my fucked-up upbringing, I guess.

At first I just hung around clubs, bars, boy brothels (prostitution is legal), thinking I'd make friends or something. But Dutch guys are impossible, even the hustlers. They have these childishly beautiful faces that lead you to think they'll be open and sweet and so on, but it's a fluke because they're actually closed, repressed, insecure, arrogant people, all of which makes them more devastating to me, for some reason. I've never been hornier. For months I just walked around slack-jawed and hard, since every second or third guy's perfection by my standards, but whenever I tried to begin conversations with them, they'd shut up and seem overly intellectual and chilled inside. Still, one year ago this extremely cute, sleepy-eyed guy about twenty-one came on to me at an after-hours club. He said I reminded him of an American ex-boyfriend. He was a ditsy, androgynous angel with brown hair, brown eyes, and big lips, just like every guy I've ever fallen for, including you. I forget his name. Call him Jan. When we got back here, Jan couldn't believe I actually lived in a windmill, the ultimate Dutch cliché. He found that hilarious. I toured him through the little brewery, which I'm allowed to keep an emergency key to. There's not much to see, just these four stinky tanks with open tops. After a while Jan said the smell was like sex, so we went back upstairs. He was tall, skinny, big-boned. He didn't smell very much, even inside his asshole. I've always been heavily into rimming. I got that from you, as you probably know. What's rimming about? I can't tell. I'm too obsessed. Anyway, I got wilder about Jan all during the sex, instead of more tired and bored like you're supposed to. It seemed really late. I think I was fucking him dog-style. He was stunning. I think he was moaning. I was about to come. I picked up an empty beer bottle without even thinking and hit the guy over the head. I don't know why. The thing broke. He fell off the futon. My cock slid out. He shit all over my legs and the bed on his way to the floor, which made me weirdly furious. I grabbed hold of his neck and ground the broken bottle into his face, really twisting and shoving it in. Then I crawled across the room and sat cross-legged, watching him bleed to death. I stayed there all night, worn out, vaguely wondering why I didn't go phone the police, or feel guilt or sympathy for his friends. I guess I'd fantasized killing a boy for so long that all the truth did was fill in details. The feeling was already planned and decided for ten years at least. I've never felt less than amazed and relieved about the whole incident. Hours passed. At some point I dragged Jan upstairs to the top of the mill. There's a smallish room shaped like a bell that nobody's gone into for hundreds of years or whatever. I stuffed him inside and washed the stairs, floor. Whatever's left of the body is there. I've never checked. I'm not interested in a dead body's smell, no matter how cute it was. Nothing smells rotten down here, probably because of the brewery, like I said.

About three months later I killed a young boy who was hanging around outside the mill for some reason. He looked about fifteen, but he could have been anything up to twenty-one since the Dutch look like kids for a long time. Then, overnight, they turn into old hags. It's weird. I'd been smoking marijuana all day, so I was really relaxed. I found him standing in front of the door, looking up at the wheel, which doesn't revolve anymore and is locked into place. I asked if he spoke any English. He did, but not well. It was 8-ish P.M. Workers leave the brewery around 5, so I asked if he wanted to see it. He said yeah. He was thin and stoop-shouldered with spiked black hair, like a lot of Dutch kids, wearing loose pastel-colored clothes, which is standard attire here. I showed him around, then I led him upstairs. He didn't say much or seem all that interested. We shared my last beer. He must have wanted to ask about what it's like in the United States, but he was too insecure about his English, I guess. I was starving for him. I can't remember why, except that he was particularly angelic. He must have noticed my hard-on. My pants were all bulged out, etc. I asked if he was a rich kid, which made him laugh. Then I asked if he needed some money. He looked at his shoes. I offered him 500 guilders (about $250) to take off his pants and let me lick his asshole. He snorted, still watching his shoes. I asked if he understood. He nodded. I said it wouldn't take long and he needn't get hard if he didn't feel up to it. He snorted again. I decided to just sit there staring at him. Eventually he muttered, 500 guilders. His voice was high-pitched but very flat, like he was answering stupid questions all the time. I said, Sure. Then he shrugged. I asked him to strip. I stood a ways off to make him more comfortable. He took off everything but his undershirt, I don't know why. Would he rather lie down on his stomach or back? He said his back, and stretched out. I folded him into a ball, knees around his ears, weight on his shoulders, and told him to say if it hurt. When he answered, Okay, I decided to kill him for some reason. Then I got so emotionally weird that I almost broke down. I licked his ass for a couple of minutes, half sobbing. He didn't notice. I do this thing where I wet down two fingers and slide them into an asshole then move them apart so the hole opens up all the way to the rectum. I lean over and sniff someone's bowels, I don't know why. This kid's was rank. I closed it up right away. He shut his eyes and let out regular breaths through his nose. I worked my hands under his shirt, which he didn't notice or mind. I played with his nipples. When that made him grin just the tiniest bit, I thought, Fuck it, why not, and grabbed his neck. He opened his eyes very wide. Otherwise he didn't fight me at all. It takes a lot longer to strangle someone than you'd think. At some point his eyes changed. They got kind of empty, fake. I noticed that diarrhea had squirted out of his ass, trickling all down his back. It smelled gruesome. When he was definitely a corpse, I ran over and leaned out a window. Occasionally I'd check to see if he'd moved. He hadn't. He looked so beautiful with his eyes empty, I don't know why. I walked back to the futon, sat down, and gazed into their glassiness a long, long time, daydreaming and numb. I didn't know what to do next, with his body I mean, so I kept it around for a few days pushed up against one of the walls. His skin got this weird dusky color. It was a very rough winter. Maybe that's why he didn't smell the whole time. I had a million ideas how I wanted to carve up and study the kid. I couldn't do it, I don't know why. Eventually I dragged him outside late one night and threw him into a canal that runs by the windmill, assuming somebody would find him and I'd be arrested. I don't know what actually happened because he was never reported either missing or dead in the papers or anything, as far as I can tell.

What's weird is he didn't fight back. He just accepted death. Every single time I've killed a Dutch boy this happens. It must be a part of the problem that makes them so cold and un-knowable in general. They're like rabbits, at least in the sense that when a rabbit gets scared it freezes up. You can threaten to kick it, it won't move. If one of these boys ever actually fought with me now, I'd probably have a brain hemorrhage I'd be so shocked.

I just realized that if you're still reading you must be the person I want you to be. God, I hope so.

After the second time I got more methodical. That's been facilitated by these two German murderer guys. Jorg and Ferdinand live in a squat not far away from the mill. They're as fucked up as I am, just not as intelligent. They kill guys because it's a kick, whereas for me it's religious or something. I met them at a bar. Germans are more knowable than the Dutch. So I was talking drunkenly about the idea of murder to them and they told me they'd strangled somebody, a drunk, in Köln. That's why they'd moved here to Holland, supposedly. They seemed really calm about things. When I was sure they were cool, I just casually mentioned the two boys I'd killed. They seemed amazed. They wanted to hear every detail. We officially joined forces that night, shook on it, all that. Since they basically don't give a shit who they kill just as long as it's gory, I get to handpick most of our victims and pretty much how the death happens. So I'm much more imaginative and violent now. They're big, muscly guys in their late twenties, but Ferdinand looks younger. Neither guy is particularly cute.

The weekend I met them we killed a guy who worked part-time at a fish market right near their squat. He was a typical Dutch yuppie guy who acted overly snotty whenever they came in to shop. They're kind of scruffy. Luckily for me he was almost my type. Except he was a dishwater blond and had a very light mustache. Stores usually close at 5 P.M.; Tuesdays they're open till 10. He worked on Tuesdays with some older guy. Ferdinand, Jorg, and I drank at a bar up the street. Jorg has a fierce-looking pistol he carries around in his belt. When the fish market closed, the yuppie strolled up the street, past the bar, toward a bus stop. We followed him for a while. Then Jorg yelled, Let's do it. We ran. Jorg put the gun in the boy's back. It was weird, very crime movie. Ferdinand told him to shut up. He stiffened. We walked him rapidly toward the mill. An elderly couple walked by. I don't think we registered in their eyes. He didn't try to escape for some reason. As soon as we got him upstairs, Ferdinand and Jorg started punching and slapping him. They said it was "payback" for treating them shittily at the store. All he did was breathe hard and look frustrated. Jorg broke the yuppie's nose. At least it sounded that way. They kicked every part of his body. As a favor I stood around letting them get their frustrations out. Still, they fucked up the guy pretty bad. It wasn't uninteresting to watch, except I started to feel sympathetic toward him, which could be a problem someday. So I never let them go crazy again. He didn't fight or yell out, which was the most extreme case of the rabbit-syndrome thing I've ever seen. I don't know if it was pride or whatever. He was semi-unconscious when they quit the battering, etc. At my request, they dragged him onto the futon and cut off his clothes with a Swiss army knife, "accidentally" stabbing him lightly here and there. The guy's eyes were rolling around in his head. Once he was naked the Germans went over and stood by the fridge. They opened a couple of beers and started blabbing in German. The guy was all bruised and sliced up, but cute nevertheless, though I've seen better bodies. His legs were too hairy. So was the crack of his ass. The buttocks were saggy and thick. He had the faint beginnings of a beer belly. I rolled him onto his stomach and buried my face in his ass for a while. Jorg yelled, Hey Dennis, and threw me the knife. I stabbed the buttocks a couple of times. They didn't bleed. I rolled him over, pulled down my pants, and rubbed my ass on his face, which drove the Germans insane. They chanted, Shit, shit, shit. So I did, directly onto his mouth, stabbing his thighs every once in a while. Jorg ran over and stomped the shit into his face. I heard more stuff break in his head. I asked if they thought he was dead. Ferdinand asked if I wanted that. I said, Okay. Ferdinand picked up a kitchen knife, Jorg took the Swiss army knife, and they stabbed his chest, making "oof" noises. He bled really wildly. He had to be dead after that. I was standing there watching them, jerking off, when something weird happened that never reoccurred. Jorg came over, knelt down, and sucked my cock deep into his throat. I came in his head. I even thought I loved Jorg for the next day or two, though he acted like nothing had happened between us. Still, at that moment, for whatever reason, Jorg was starved for my sperm. Weird. Anyway, they grabbed the guy's body and dragged it downstairs, yelling how they knew a burial spot and they'd see me tomorrow. I spent all night cleaning the place. They buried the corpse by their squat, apparently. I thought that was risky. Still, we've never heard anything, so I guess it's okay.

We've killed two other boys. The first was this punk, maybe twenty, twenty-one, whom I'd seen around town, always wearing the same filthy coat with the names of heavy metal bands scribbled all over it. Seeing him would make me ache for a couple of days, sometimes longer. Before I met Ferdinand and Jorg he seemed so impossible. But one afternoon I was walking around with the Germans when he came the

opposite way, holding onto this one particular punk girl as
always. I told the Germans I wanted to kill him. I'd learned
how to say that without any feeling at all. Ferdinand said,
That's no problem. It turned out the punk lived in their squat.
They thought he was arrogant, stupid, pretentious, ugly, etc.,
so they were happy to help. They told me they'd just casually
mention to him how they knew somebody who lived in a
windmill. He'd definitely want a tour, they said. They'd try to
coax him to visit that night. When we split off, I bought some
rope so we could tie him if need be. They came by around 11
P.M. We opened beers, sat around. He listened more than he
talked. I asked if he wanted a tour. He said, Okay. I showed
him the tanks. At one point he strolled off alone, and I told
Jorg and Ferdinand to wait for my signal. Ferdinand said I was
obviously in love with the guy so no problem. The punk
thought the brewery was cool. We went back upstairs, drank
more beer. I was totally in awe. At one point I managed to ask,
Are you gay? He said no but he didn't mind gays. I asked if
he'd ever had sex with another guy. He said no, very blasé
about it. I asked if he'd ever thought about fucking with gay
men for money. He said yeah once. Ferdinand and Jorg sat
there watching. I said, How about now with us? He laughed.
Seriously? he asked. I said, Sure. He asked how much. I said,
You tell us. He said, 300 guilders plus two bags of heroin,
which we had to score for him. I said, Fine. That kind of
shocked him, I think. He leaned back and said, Oh, so that's
what this bullshit's about. I said yeah. Then Jorg and Ferdinand left to score heroin. The boy said he had his own needle.
We were alone, with him cross-legged facing me on the futon,
acting like he knew he drove me totally insane. He asked a few
questions, then nodded at the answers. I told him I'd wanted
to fuck him for months, which made him look even more full
of himself. I said, You've obviously done this before. He said
yeah but we were lucky we'd asked when he was broke. The
Germans came back with dope. He shot up. Then he stretched

out on the floor by the fridge, very peaceful and pale, mumbling. I said, Let's move to the bed. He sort of staggered across the room, dropped facedown on the futon. Stand him up, I said, Strip him. The Germans hoisted him up to his feet. First he said, Hey, what the fuck are you doing? Then he gave up and said, Oh okay. His clothes only looked complicated. They were a coat, T-shirt, pants, all of which slid right off. I said, Leave his boots on, I don't know why. His body was flawless—white, smooth, hard, dime nipples, big cock, dangly balls, square ass, hairless crack. He'd started nodding like junkies do. Hold him up, I said. I moved in close, feeling his body, especially his ass, which was so cold and soft. I told him I wanted to do everything that was humanly possible to him. He didn't say anything. He's too stoned, Jorg said. I asked Ferdinand, Will he fall if you guys let him go? They nodded. So let him go. They did. He collapsed on the floor and started groaning, but I don't think he was actually hurt. I stripped, knelt down next to his face and put my cock against his lips. I said, Suck. He opened his mouth. I started fucking it. That looked fantastic. At one point I stopped and french-kissed him, telling him how much I worshiped him. He was rubbing my back or my head while I did this. I licked down his body, tried sucking his cock. It wouldn't get hard, which made me furious for some reason. I don't know what I expected. I climbed off and told Jorg to kick the guy once in the stomach. He did. The guy balled up, retching. I told Jorg to hand me his gun. I pointed it at the guy's forehead. Open your eyes, I said, I'm going to kill you. He mumbled, No, no, no. The Germans came over and tied his wrists, ankles. Ferdinand said we should put something into his mouth. I thought he was saying my cock so I buried it. He probably meant a gag, but it's soundproof in here as far as anyone can tell. After a while Jorg suggested we carry the boy to the basically unused third floor of the mill and dangle him from the rafters. That way we could easily fuck him around, three on one. Great idea. The Germans started untying his ankles. I watched, jerking off. He was murmuring something in Dutch. They were ready to walk him upstairs, but I told them to hold it, I wanted to eat out his ass while his body was flexible. So they laid him back down on the futon and contorted his hips until the asshole was totally accessible. They skinned back the cheeks with their fingers until it was a purple cave. I started nibbling and sucking it. I tried to blow it up like a balloon, pried it even more open, sniffed the depths, etc. The Germans thought that was ridiculous, as usual. I felt kind of lost and irrational. I'd never wanted to eat someone's shit before, but I was starved for the punk's. I asked him if it had been eaten before. He mumbled, No, let me go. I asked if he'd like me to eat it. He said, Are you really going to kill me? I said, No, very casually. Then I repeated my question. He said he didn't know what I meant. I said if he'd shit in my mouth we'd let him go. He said okay. He sounded totally exhausted. His ass looked fantastic. I stared at the thing for a few seconds. Then I put my hand under the hole. The punk looked terrified but kind of haughty. I think Dutch faces must have some haughtiness built into them or whatever. His neck was all crumpled up under his chin like a walrus's. I said, Shit. He contorted his face. A long shit squirted out. I had to move my hand around quickly to catch it all. I was so wild for the guy's looks in general that the smell hardly registered, but the Germans backed off and hooted, so it probably stank really bad. I started eating it. The Germans watched me, fascinated, I think, but pretending to puke and etc. It tasted okay, kind of bland. I swallowed three mouthfuls, then wiped off the rest on the floor and licked his asshole clean, inside, out. Then I said, Ferdinand, Jorg, take the idiot upstairs. He couldn't believe it. They grabbed him. He yelled, No, no, no. After we got him upstairs, the Germans threw a rope over a beam in the rafters. They untied his hands and retied them clasped over his head. Then they connected the two ropes and hoisted him until his feet were a foot off the floor. I stood nearby, jerking off. His face was scrunched up in discomfort, at the strain on his arms or whatever. It seemed religious, I don't know why. It also reminded me of a punching bag, like boxers use. Anyway, I was tired, so I told the Germans, Let's go downstairs for a while. The downstairs smelled gruesome, so Ferdinand opened the windows. I cleaned up the shit. We drank a few beers. The smell went away or we got used to it. There was no noise at all from upstairs, as far as we could tell. I asked Ferdinand and Jorg what they'd do with the punk if they could. They said what I knew they'd say, Beat him to death. I understood how that would be great and everything, but it wasn't enough somehow, at least for me. So I told them to go home, sleep, and we'd meet up the next day and finish the boy off, once I'd had some time to decide. They said, Fine, left. I was too tense to sleep. So I went back upstairs late that night and just watched the punk hang there. At first he didn't notice me. Then he said, Let me go, I won't tell, etc. I said, No, his death was important to me. He couldn't possibly understand, I said. Even I didn't understand, really. He tried to discuss it with me intellectually. I said it wasn't a rational thing, he might as well give up. Then I caressed him all over. It was like I was frisking him, only much more extensively. All he said the whole time was his back hurt, almost to himself. I examined it. I couldn't tell what was the problem. So I knelt down and licked out his ass again, finger-fucked it. The fingering made him scream, because it put too much stress on his muscles, I guess. When he screamed his mouth opened incredibly wide. Then I really wanted to kill him. The red mouth triggered the need, because it was a preview or something. I went downstairs, came back up with the kitchen knife. He whispered, No, no, no, when he saw it. I said, Everything is over. I don't know why I said those particular words, but they seemed to communicate what I was feeling. I asked, Did he know it was over? He said, Yes, very flatly. I told him he was the most extraordinary and beautiful boy I'd ever seen in my life and that killing him would be incredible and that he should understand how profound his death was and that I would remember his murder forever. He just looked at me. I couldn't read his expression. My hands were totally trembling, but I took the knife and aimed it at his chest about the point where his heart would have been. He looked down to see where I'd aimed, by reflex, I guess. I shoved the blade about five inches into his chest with both hands. His eyes closed. He bit his bottom lip. His head dropped back. Blood poured out around the knife, down his body. I pulled out the knife and made a light horizontal cut across his stomach, which dribbled more blood. I stretched out his penis and tried to saw it in two. I only got through a fraction of it, it was so tough. I knelt down behind him and licked his asshole but that seemed kind of pointless with him dead, so I stabbed his back a bunch of times, kissing and licking his neck as I did. Then I walked back downstairs, dressed, went out, and called the Germans, waking them up. They hurried over. They kicked the corpse around for a while. That created a pretty hilarious fireworks display of blood, with him swinging around like the clapper in an invisible bell. I wanted the Germans to cut off his head for some reason, so they severed the rope suspending him and turned the corpse on its stomach. They sawed through its neck—carving, hacking, abrading, etc. The head came free, which took a very long time. Then they kicked the headless torso around. We were all soaked with blood, not to mention a clear goo that came from some organ inside him. I felt unbelievably tired and sat down against one wall, watching them dance around. When none of us cared about the corpse anymore, the Germans picked it up by the armpits and started downstairs. It had basically run out of blood. It didn't leave much of a mess on the stairs, just some smears where its feet dragged. They left the head behind resting on one ear. It continued to hold this incredible allure, but in a weird way, obviously, since it didn't mean much anymore. Jorg came back up for it shortly. I stood at the top of the stairs and watched the punk's body go. I couldn't see the head because it was under Jorg's arm, I think. Supposedly they weighted the corpse down with pieces of concrete and dropped it into the canal. Then I stashed the hypodermic and heroin in the refrigerator. The rest is a blur. For some reason this death is the one that has weirded me out more than any other. It's not an emotional thing, more a sleepiness that wasn't there before he died. It went on for weeks afterward and is still kind of here. I kept thinking I saw the punk places, in the far edges of my eyes, and so on. I never saw the punk's girlfriend again. Maybe the Germans killed her when I wasn't around since I know that Ferdinand, at least, was attracted to her. I should ask them.

We've killed one other boy. He was ten or eleven years old. This was two weeks ago. I chose him. I think the Germans felt weird about killing a kid, but they did it. He'd been haunting me for a long time, maybe six months. He worked with his father or uncle or someone like that in a hamburger stand near the windmill. He deep-fried potatoes, turned hamburgers over, etc., while his dad manned the counter. He was always there, working or sitting around reading comic books. He was skinny and girlish with pink cheeks, brown eyes, and long, wild hair. Something about how laconic he seemed drove me wild, not to mention his looks. I took the Germans to see him one day. They said they'd help, so we hung around until the stand closed at 6. The kid helped his dad sponge up grease and so on for a while. Then he kissed the man's cheek and strolled down the street swinging his arms, balancing on a crack in the sidewalk like kids do. We followed. The dad didn't notice us. Luckily the kid turned down a narrow street with boarded-up buildings on one side, elevated train tracks on the other. Jorg and Ferdinand ran ahead and wrestled him to the ground, which didn't take much effort, obviously. By the time I caught up, Jorg was waving his knife at the kid, who was blinking and sniffling. You understand? Jorg was saying. The kid shook his head. Jorg said the kid's English sucked. I said, Let's get him home quickly. They yanked him up to his feet, then we hustled along. I think an old man spotted us and realized something was wrong, but he didn't actually see us go into the windmill, thank God. Up, up, up, Ferdinand said, lifting the kid by his shirt collar. I was behind, Jorg in front. The kid's shirt had raised up. The small of his back was incredibly skinny and white. I stroked it a little, then slid my palm into his pants. His ass was so little and perfect it felt more like a prototype than a real ass, which made me think about what you once said about Kevin's ass, that it was a "toy ass." Actually, the kid looked a little like Kevin did then. Anyway, he kept looking startled over his shoulder at me. Upstairs Ferdinand threw the kid across the room really hard. He hit a wall and slid down to the floor. He started crying. I knelt beside him and tried to kiss, but he hid his face in the crook of one arm. I shook his shoulder. Kiss me, I said. He tried to pull away. I grabbed his head, slammed it against the wall. After that he stopped crying and looked very dazed. I dragged him toward the futon by one wrist, which was easier to do than it sounds since he didn't weigh much. Jorg said, Let us know when you need us. Okay. I laid the kid out on his back, unbuttoned his shirt, took it off, unzipped his short pants, and gave them a yank. He didn't wear underpants or have pubic hair yet. His genitals were too tiny to be very interesting. I put my lips close to his face and whispered, I love you, baby. I really felt like I did. You understand? I asked. He shook his head. It's true, I said. I undressed. The Germans stood by the refrigerator, as usual, drinking, half paying attention. The kid watched me intently, eyes fixed on my hard-on. I couldn't read their expression. I knelt over his face, aimed my cock at his mouth. His eyes were still fixed on the head of my cock, vaguely cross-eyed by that point, because it was so close. I thought that looked sexy, I don't know why. I dabbed a little drop of pre-come on his lips, smearing it around with my thumb. I forced the thumb inside his mouth, even deep down his throat. Then I brought it out coated with spit and smeared his lips again. I pushed in my cock. I couldn't fit much inside. The difference was too great. When I forced it he started to squeal. So the Germans rushed up with a long piece of rope and tied the kid's hands in case he decided to struggle, though like I said, Dutch guys don't fight back, period. Physically, anyway. Ferdinand got out the heroin and cooked it up in a spoon. He shot it into a vein behind one of the kid's knees. It took effect right away. The kid's squeals sort of faded. He sounded more like a cat mewing. His eyes rolled back in his head, but he wasn't OD'ing, according to Ferdinand, who seemed to know. Still we kept his wrists tied in case. The Germans went back to the fridge. The kid looked more beautiful than before. It had something to do with the mildly lush build of his body combined with that sort of erased angel face. I leaned over and french-kissed his mouth for a while, sucking juice from his lips, biting them until they leaked a little blood, sucking that, then finger-fucking his throat. The next time I rammed my cock down there and managed to get half inside. But it came out coated with blood, which I scraped on a finger and licked. I slapped his face five, six, seven times. It turned scarlet. I fucked it some more, gripping him by the ears. I screwed his face all the way down my cock, until his nostrils were full of my pubic hair. Then I pulled out, cradled his head in one hand, and punched his face with the other. It was bleeding furiously from the lip and nose. I squeezed his throat, banged the back of his head against the floor. I'm almost sure I heard the Germans laughing. Afterward he was still breathing, just raspily. I licked every inch of him from the callused soles of his feet to the part in his hair. He tasted amazingly sweet and mild. Someone once told me young boys taste like nuts. He sort of did. I probably would have paid hundreds to fuck him, much less to murder him. I got so impressed at one point I lay my head on his ass and let his taste kind of melt in my mouth. Jorg, I want to open him up, I mumbled. He came over and squatted nearby, handing me the Swiss army knife. I rolled the kid over, cut his ropes. I pressed the point of the blade into the base of his throat and made a long, straight slit all the way down his chest, stomach. It wasn't deep enough, so I went over it again. This time I managed to part a small area between his nipples and see maybe two inches square of purple material. I licked all inside there. It was incredibly lush. Blood was leaking from five or six spots along the cut. I wish he could see this, I said. He's too fucked up, Jorg said. I went over the cut once more. It opened up. I pulled back the halves of white stomach flesh and saw his jumbled yellow guts, which had a weird strong stench. His chest was still rising and falling. That fascinated me for some reason, so I punched his face several more times. Then I deep-tongued his slobbery mouth for a while. I was really delirious. I gave Jorg the knife. Cut him more open, I said. I concentrated on kissing, while Jorg hacked away in my peripheral vision. I tried to induce vomiting with my fingers. His system was too broken down by that point or whatever. When I looked up, Jorg was trying to carve off the kid's left leg. I watched that for a while. It didn't work for some reason. Blood was just barreling out of the area. Ferdinand was leaning over Jorg's shoulder. The kid's insides were much more science-fictional than I imagined. Still, there was something so ugly and earthy about them. I could understand why they were meant to be hidden away. Anyway it made me more curious about his ass, which I hadn't explored yet for some reason. Wait, I said. Jorg quit carving. We tipped the kid onto his side. At that, guts sloshed out of the stomach wound onto the futon. Jorg sat there staring down at the organs in shock. Ferdinand couldn't believe it. He reeled away, shouting something in German. I asked Jorg, Is the kid still alive? He didn't think it was possible. I didn't care all that much anymore. I wiped the blood off his ass as best I could, grabbed the calf of his one intact leg and bent it way forward, opening the ass-crack. I licked it out for a long time, while Jorg hacked the rest of the body in ways I could feel more than see. The kid was rocking around like an earthquake. I felt totally at peace. His hole tasted metallic. I stretched it open and sniffed. The bowels reeked as harshly as I've ever known. I spat on the hole and fucked it brutally, which wasn't easy. The thing was a pinhole. Jorg kept stabbing the corpse kind of lazily. Then I got an idea. Stomp the kid's head, I said. Jorg jumped up, did. It was really horrific. The back of the head just caved in. The hair got all goopy with blood and brain tissue or something. Jorg pulled down his pants and dropped some shit on the crushed head. It was facedown by this point. Turn the corpse over, I said. He did. The face was still beautiful, smiling, which I couldn't believe. So the Germans and I got together and stomped until his face wasn't human. That made cracking and gurgling sounds. We rolled the corpse onto its stomach. I enlarged the asshole with the Swiss army knife and worked one of my hands to the wrist inside. It was wild in there, like reaching into a stew that had started to cool. But it was tight too, a glove or whatever. The Germans were carving their names in the corpse, laughing. I pumped my hand in and out of the ass feeling weirdly furious, with the dead kid I guess. Then we cut him apart for a few hours, and studied everything inside the body, not saying much to one another, just the occasional, Look at this, or swear word, until there was nothing around but a big, off-white shell in the middle of the worst mess in the world. God, human bodies are such garbage bags. We fell asleep curled on the floor. I didn't wake up until late the next day. When I opened my eyes, Ferdinand and Jorg were scooping up parts of the kid in their hands and plopping them into plastic bags. The futon was ruined. I bought a new one. The floor's still blackish from where the kid's blood soaked into the wood. We'd demolished him to the extent that there was no sense of what he'd looked like in the pieces of him that were left. It was like we'd erased him. It's weird. None of us can remember his looks in any detail. When I try to picture him, I just go blind and my cock gets unbelievably hard.

Now you know. Here's what I'm hoping—you're who I believe you are, which means I hope you're like me, because we used to be so much alike, right? Trust me. I want you to live here with me and participate in this discovery, like we used to do in our teens, but with this major transcendence or answer I've found in killing cute guys. The Germans have gone to Portugal or somewhere for a while. So it'd be you and me. We'll do it ourselves. It's totally easy. Nothing's happened to me. I feel strong, powerful, clear all the time. Nothing bothers me anymore. I'm telling you, Julian, this is some kind of ultimate truth. Come on, do it. Am I wrong about you? Write to me care of the American Express office in Amsterdam.

Dennis

DENNIS. DON'T DO ANYTHING UNTIL I GET THERE. ARRIVING BY TRAIN 8 PM FRIDAY. BRINGING KEVIN WHO'S STAYING WITH ME. MEET US. JULIAN.

WILDER

1 9 8 9

Kevin glanced up from his copy of Tolkien's *The Lord of the Rings*, Book One. The train had sped two, three hundred miles since he'd last checked the view, but it looked like the same fenced-off field out there, only his face and Julian's were superimposed, and every detail, including them, was as gray as a silent film.

He kicked his brother's leg. It had wound up between his legs, resting against the right almost flirtatiously.

Julian's sunburned face spasmed, especially the mouth. "Huh?!"

"Your leg," Kevin said, lowering his eyes to the novel. This was the fifth time he'd read it. Its narrative felt like his ulterior life. There was a snapshot of him at ten or eleven years old with it perched in his lap. His eyes, which only seconds before had been deep in the novel, were fixed on the lens and resembled silvery, glistening caves to another dimension or some-

108

thing. He thought so. The shot belonged in one of those "unexplained phenomena" books, next to a crude little sketch of a UFO.

He read for a while, extremely lost, happy, etc.

He looked at himself in the glass again. It was so dark outside that an orangy reflection of Julian, him, the insides of the train, had superseded the view. Kevin's eyes looked messed-up in a positive way, like people's on Ecstacy. The train, other passengers, were just sort of there, a backdrop. Julian seemed nervous. No, not seemed, *was*. Nervous. Kevin closed the book around a finger.

"What are you thinking about?" he said, swiveling in the seat to see the real world. It looked less exquisite than it had in the glass, much less than it did all dolled-up in the book.

"Dennis, naturally," Julian said, resting his forehead against the window/mirror. "Whether he'll actually meet us at the station. What he looks like now. Whether visiting him isn't totally insane under the circumstances. Why we're here. On this train, I mean. I don't mean why we exist, obviously." He sat up, grinned. The grin thinned immediately. "You look sort of . . . I don't know, carefree or something."

Kevin sniffed. "It's this book," he said, opening, reentering it. "I'm . . . half with you, half . . . in here. It's . . . hard . . . to . . ." Tolkien's language began to affect him again. ". . . uh . . ." He forgot the train. Actually, a fraction of his eyes still registered it in a way, because he could sense his brother staring off, then watching him, then glancing around the compartment. But most of his thoughts trailed a handful of tiny, humanesque men around a sinister forest.

Gradually, like a filmic dissolve, his mind paved the fictional woods with that image of him at ten or eleven, his eyes full of Tolkien's fog. Perhaps, as Julian claimed, his face was just too near the lens and, so, slightly unfocused, but even if that was true, fate had unfocused him, he thought. Because it was the only great shot ever taken of him, or the only one where he wasn't compromised by the prettiness he felt so much ennui about. "Shoot." He'd just read three pages without learning anything. He folded the corner of page 121, shut the book.

A teenaged boy walked through the car. He was baby-faced, stoop-shouldered, six foot plus, wearing loose-fitting pale raspberry clothes, which only contributed to the sense that he was sleepwalking. From the loaded expression on Julian's fast-turning head, the teen obviously met some criteria of beauty. So Kevin checked him out too, or tried to at least, since he could never evaluate other cute people. He could only take sides, meaning theirs over people's who weren't cute. In this case the young brunet's, since at thirty-three, Julian wasn't particularly cute anymore.

The door at the end of the car shut behind the teen.

Julian untwisted his neck, smiled wistfully in Kevin's direction. "What's his story, Kev? I know he's not hot in the conventional sense, and I'm sure . . . well, *pretty* sure if he was naked I'd yawn, but those clothes, that slight hunch, that spacey expression, those cut-glass features . . . *something* there's devastating. You just want to . . . I don't know what exactly. I'm not saying kill him, à la Dennis. Fuck him, eat him out, absolutely. But it's also got some sort of . . . ethereal quality? Or no, less lofty than that. It's more like—"

"*Amsterdam Centraal Station,*" announced a distorted voice. "*Einde punt van deze trein.*"

Kevin shielded his eyes, pressed his face to the window. Amsterdam's skyline reminded him of a dessert tray. It was lighted so carefully, period detail after period detail, in such myriad of colors, Kevin wondered if it was being photographed for a children's storybook that evening. Or, if not, gee, what sort of people would live in there? He pictured friendly, bewhiskered, blond, diminutive types wearing quaint uniforms with a very slight fakeness around the collars and cuffs, like Disneyland employees. Just then the dirty glass wall of the station slid between him and that interpretation.

"Kev, hurry!" Julian disappeared through the sliding door.

By the time Kevin caught up, his brother was already out on the platform, talking with the teen they'd seen earlier. The teen looked dazedly at the back of Julian's hand, saying his telephone number in a weird accent, watching the digits appear on the skin in a craggy blue script.

"Please call, okay?" The teen smiled, waved, blended into a crowd of similarly dressed, equally tall people.

Kevin, Julian roamed the platform studying male faces. They didn't recognize any. No one registered them, aside from the usual gay men wiped out by Kevin's prettiness. Yawn. Julian raced off to check the crannies of the station. Kevin slouched on a bench on the platform, hugging his knapsack, head tipped back, thinking how palacelike the glass roof looked. He wondered what little changes he'd make if someone were to give the train station to him as a gift. Like would he clean off the soot up there, or leave the sky that swirly, dreamy brown? He was trying to make up his mind when he sensed someone eyeing him off to his left and turned, expecting to see the usual leering, mustachioed male.

It was obviously me. My brown hair had faded to dark gray. Fuller face. The same studiedly casual clothes. Bigger nose than he remembered. Same eyes. "Kevin?" Same voice. "Hey, it's you, right!?" I yelled. Kevin nodded solemnly. "You look unbelievable! Jesus! Where's your brother?!"

"Hunting for you," Kevin squeaked. He was practically strangling his knapsack. Weird. "You look, uh, nice too." He tried to recall how positive he'd been back in Paris, and how strenuously he had argued with Julian that my letter was fiction. At the same time he tried hard to loosen his grip on the knapsack but couldn't quite manage it.

I sat down beside him. "Kevin, I'm so glad you could . . ." Kevin smiled desperately at the far wall of the station, willing

Julian to reappear at that instant. "... amazing discoveries I'm making about..." He could feel the small, fat rectangle of *The Lord of the Rings*, Book One, through the plasticesque fabric of the knapsack. "... because you won't believe how I can..." He gripped the rectangle like it was J.R.R. Tolkien's hand.

"Dennis?" Julian traced my line of sight to Kevin's body. He'd drifted to sleep on my futon. "... uh ..." Following the sightline more carefully, Julian came to his brother's ass. Ugh. "Listen, man," he whispered. "I understand the appeal. I mean of killing some guy you've completely objectified. Sure, sure. I can picture it. It's crossed my mind. Not as elaborately as it crosses yours. Still, you're actually murdering guys, and I'm not being moralistic. I'm talking fairness, which is not a particularly bad rule to live by, as rules go." He raised his voice. "You *know*?"

Sniffle. Kevin's head left the pillow, raised a foot, and gazed blearily at Julian. The lower half of his face had turned a moist purplish-pink with scraggly indentations; the upper half was the usual. If Opie, the kid on the old "Andy Griffith Show," had grown up cute like he was obviously supposed to, and not gotten chubby and bald like the actor who'd played him, he could have been Kevin's twin, minus a few million freckles. "Sorry, Kev," Julian said, grinning. Kevin lowered back down into sleep. "So, Dennis ..." I was still studying the ass. "... why don't we take this conversation upstairs, *eh*?"

Julian couldn't get over how otherworldly the windmill felt. The lower of my two floors was quite spartan, if livable, an arklike UFO. The upper floor, which he and I were touring at that moment, was a little bit smaller and extraordinarily dusty. Parts of the floorboards were stained with a black substance, shimmery as a dance floor, presumably dehydrated blood. Some young punk's, if Julian remembered the letter right. So these were the rafters the punk had supposedly dangled from, spewing stuff. Julian leaped up, grabbed one, did a few wobbly chin-ups.

Then he dangled there, spacing. I circled the wooden room, fingering my temples. Once, years ago, Julian had believed in some theory that criminal types had a black aura, halfway between a cloud and veil, which covered their whole bodies—six, seven, eight inches thick. In the right kind of drug state, the theory went, one could spot this covering. Julian squinted. I just seemed older, uh . . . thicker, less sexy somehow, but no more physically dark than any thirty-three-year-old in inadequate light. Maybe my walk was too stumbly, or, uh . . . Shit. I'd stopped circling, turned, and glared up at him.

"What's your verdict?" I mumbled. Julian dropped to the floor, lost his balance. *Thud . . . thud, thud.* "I think," he said, clambering to his feet. ". . . I think you remember our friendship selectively. Either that or I've changed a lot, which I doubt, though Kevin says I have too. Changed, I mean. Because that thing we used to do with the three-ways was drug-induced youth shit, before I knew what I wanted in life, which, it turns out, is your traditional gay relationship with occasional affairs to keep myself alert. Anyway, no, I'm not interested. Sorry." He felt immediately guilty.

"But, uh, Kevin's always had this obsession with you, so maybe . . ." He froze. "Jesus! *What* am I *saying*? Shit. Forget that. Besides, Kevin thinks your letter's bullshit. I don't know what *I* believe, but I *will* say it's strange how you stare at him. At Kevin. It reads as desire, but under the circumstances, what's that to you? Because desire and violence seem inseparable, if I'm reading that letter right. I realize Kevin's cute. I've objectified him all my life in different ways. But he's my brother, which overrides everything technically. Point is, one, no, I won't help, and, two, lay off Kevin, man!"

I shrugged, nodded. My eyes looked kind of drugged. Amphetamine, maybe. Julian didn't know how else to place the tinniness of my expression. It didn't seem crazy exactly, at least not in the way actors' faces would suddenly lose it, explode. It was just a bit off, which is why he thought drugs, i.e., distortion, but ... "It's the weirdest fucking thing, Julian," I muttered. "About Kevin. He reminds me of something I felt before I stopped feeling anything. Pre-desire, pre-violence. That sounds ridiculous, I know. But I can't imagine it actually is, is it? Shit." I swayed in Julian's mind.

Something woke Kevin. It wasn't the voices upstairs, which resembled a clumsy drum solo, at least to his focusing ears. He hadn't sprung from a nightmare, because he either didn't have dreams or he never remembered them. Maybe he day-dreamed so much that his brain used bedtime to take mini-vacations. He'd lie down, switch off, *click, hiss* ... That's how he imagined it. So what could have woken him? Maybe the windmill was haunted. He was positive the things in my letter were fiction, but say if they weren't, and there were these cute young ghosts drifting around in the mill in another dimension. He yawned, squinted, scanned the place. Nothing. "Shoot." So he made one up. A boy who looked like he did at ten or eleven, but transparent, frail, stooped, melancholy, whereas he'd been a bundle of nerves. Kevin made the "boy" float over shyly, hands behind his back, and announce in a wispy voice (this was the hard part), "Oh, I'm sorry to disturb you, sir. See, death is extraordinarily interesting and all, but sometimes, well, I get lonely." The ghost extended a see-through hand. Kevin reached out to grip it. That part was way too theatrical, he realized, for as soon as they "touched," the ghost not only vanished, it seemed like a corny idea in the first place. Besides, any ghost here would have to be nude, Kevin thought, and mutilated. He propped himself up on his elbows and tried again. The same "boy" drew close, nude this time, his hands cupping his genitals. Kevin had never seen anyone seriously hurt, so he just made the "boy's" chest look shredded, using as his model a painting by Rembrandt that some nut had slashed with a knife in some poorly attended museum. Cool, he thought, admiring his work. "Say something." The "boy" shuddered. "Don't be afraid," Kevin added. "I made you up, after all." The "boy" sat down gingerly on the edge of the futon. He seemed about to cry. Kevin smiled sympathetically, remembering not to try to touch the ghost, no matter how appropriate it seemed, lest—

"Tell me about *him*," the "boy" said, grimacing at the ceiling. He had a voice much like Kevin's own, though it equally resembled the sound of the little humidifier Kevin kept by his Parisian bed.

"Are you referring to Dennis?" Kevin whispered.

The "boy" nodded. "The . . . one . . . who . . . killed . . . me." He wrapped his arms around himself and looked tenderly, emptily into Kevin's eyes. The "boy's" face was swollen and bruised, but his fogginess made him as easy on the eyes as a puffy cloud.

"Dennis used to be great," Kevin said. "We were lovers when I was a kid. He'd get distant on me and kind of rough sexually, but I didn't care, even though I was miserable in general. Because Dennis listened. He respected my fantasies, probably because he has weird ones himself. Julian never cared. I had a nervous breakdown two months ago; Julian took me in, but that was pure obligation. He hates me. I drive him and his lover nuts. But I guess I'm not answering your question."

The "boy" shook his head. Maybe he'd started crying. Yeah, why not? Sure. Cool. The idea gave Kevin chills. A boy-shaped cloud raining. Weird. But how would that look? Kevin couldn't imagine. "Shoot." So he had the "boy" cover his face with his hands. "Don't cry," Kevin sighed, secretly willing the ghost to grow hysterical. Then he got an idea. "Hey," he added brightly, "tell me what it was like to be murdered by Dennis."

"Oh, it was gross," the gray boy wailed through his hands. "I—" Wait, Kevin thought. He'd have an accent or something. Start again. "It was gross," the "boy" reannounced in a coarse accent, somewhere between German and some sort of Irishy brogue. "First Dennis—" Kevin fast-forwarded him through the speech, not knowing how to describe a violent scene. Now what? He couldn't decide. Anyway, he was tired of the ghost idea. He killed it off, lay back, and stared at the splintery wooden ceiling. After an indeterminate number of bland, drifty thoughts, he stood, straightened his clothes, and scaled the mill's central, spiral staircase. It was at least ten degrees colder up where Julian and I were sitting. "Brr." Dimly lighted by one crumpled clip-lamp, the room was a lot like the other floor, only totally unfurnished, sans bathroom, and covered with dust like the bag in a huge vacuum cleaner.

"Sleep well?" I asked, startling Kevin out of a forgettable daydream.

He tiptoed across the room. "Okay, I guess. Aren't you guys freezing?"

The instant Kevin sat down, Julian jumped up, stretched, yawned in a totally phony-ass way. "I'm gonna go call that kid," he said, eyeing Kevin dismissively. "Have you got a phone, D.?"

"No, but there's one at the corner. Turn left when you go out the door. Tell the kid we're in the windmill. He'll know it. Here's the key." I fished around in a pocket, threw Julian what looked like a particle of light. "And a Dutch quarter. For the phone." Ditto.

"Who's 'kid'?" Kevin asked once Julian had split. He could see in my eyes how enamored I was with him. Still, the crush or whatever seemed kind of ironic or something, Kevin couldn't quite tell, which made it a lot less nerve-racking, though obviously, and he could never forget this, that crush shared the same brain with scary ideas like exploding boys, necrophilia, etc.

"Some boy Julian met on the train. You didn't see him?"

"Yeah."

It was as if my blue eyes had been hit with a spotlight. Each iris framed a white, upside-down, wavy teardrop. "And your verdict?" I demanded.

"First, what are you guys planning to do? I mean you're not going to murder him, right?"

I looked away. The eyeball ghosts vanished. "Julian doesn't want to. So I guess it'll just be three-way, or . . . a four-way *if* . . . " I glanced at him. "Otherwise, you can hide out up here, read . . . "

That sounded innocent enough. "Let's see," Kevin said. "Well, you want to know who the boy most reminded me of?" He could feel himself blushing. "A guy Julian and you had a three-way with millions of years ago. I used to watch you guys screw through the keyhole sometimes."

"Wh-which guy?" The light had returned to my eyes, but it was all twisted up. "I mean . . . do you remember us saying his first name was Henry?"

"No." Kevin scrunched up his forehead and tried to think, but I was acting too interested. "Gosh, let's see. Uh, he had long black hair. Skinny. He had sort of a baby face. He seemed really drugged."

"That sounds like anyone we ever slept with." My shoulders slumped, head dropped, face dangled loosely. "We had such specific tastes," I continued mournfully. "I still do. But Henry. Shit. Didn't I ever tell you about these fake snuff photographs?"

Kevin shook his head. "No, I don't think so," he said, but his memory was notoriously flaky. "Describe them to me."

*   *   *

"Dennis, you, hmm, *stand* at the foot of the futon." Julian pointed there. I lumbered over, eyes fixed on the bedding's new centerpiece, a kid's bowed head. "And, uh, Chretien?" The kid looked up from the purple shoelace he'd been fingering nervously. He looked stoned. Julian still felt a little too wowed by the kid's beauty. "You're amazing," he announced, and glanced over at me. "Very us circa 'seventy-four, 'seventy-five, right, Dennis?" "Definitely." I nodded, eyeing the kid. "He's exquisite." Chretien crinkled his nose, wiped it off with a pale purple sleeve. "And so endearing," Julian sighed. "Anyway, Perfect Young Being, could you get naked and lie on your back for us?" "Or *else*!" I added, shaking a fist.

It was like time speeded up for cheap, comic effect. Within a second or two Chretien had undressed, flung himself onto the futon, and buried his face in a pillow. Yum. "Hey, Julian!" I hissed, indicating the heap of discarded purple clothes. At their top was a perfectly circular dent like a nest, and inside it, a mock treasure trove—green chewing gum pinched in a thin paper cloud, two condoms, coins, half-smoked joint, student ID card with a scared-looking kid in one corner. Julian immediately snatched the card. "When was this photo taken?" he demanded. Chretien scrunched up his forehead. "1988," he answered in his sludgy accent.

The boy in the picture was even more stunning than Chretien himself. "D., in your letter you mentioned something about—Oh, wait, Chretien, you should be lying on your back now, okay?—about the way Dutch guys age poorly, right? Because this kid, as nice as he looks nowadays, is prettier in this picture. See?" Julian passed me the card over Chretien's chest, which was pretty much sterling. A great, complex rib cage. Maybe his nipples could be a teensy bit bigger, the shoulders, um, wider . . . "No," I said, tossing the card back, "I think in this case it's the objectified-people-look-better syndrome. Photos are perfect by nature. A kid's just, well, workable?"

"Mm," Julian said, studying Chretien with that thought in mind. "Anyway, we're starting. Are you as stoned as you want to be?" The kid's forehead crumpled. "Yes. Can you tell?" he chirped. Horrible accent. Everyone laughed simultaneously. Nice. "D., take his face. I'll . . ." Julian positioned his grin over Chretien's groin. ". . . start here. Mm." Whitish blur. My ass blocked his view of the kid's upper half. Julian bobbed for the balls. Once, twice . . . A ball oozed down the back of his tongue. "Mm." The kid's crotch smelled very faintly of . . . pecan pie? Julian opened one eye to make sure I wasn't turning psychotic.

He parted the kid's lo-o-o-ong legs. That pecanesque smell wafted up. He'd forgotten how strangely profound cute strangers' tastes, odors, looks, etc., could seem at first. And how satisfying it was to hear some cute boy's voice transcend language. "Mmrmph," Chretien said. Julian jabbed his tongue into the craggy brown asshole. "Rowph, mmrm." He jabbed, jabbed, jabbed . . . One of his watery eyes fixed on me. I seemed my old self, just older. Chretien: "Ohmglugm." Maybe Kevin was right. Julian hauled in his tongue, cleared his throat. "Having fun, Dennis?" My head jerked ambiguously. "Hey," Julian continued, motioning me over. "Maintain please. For old time's sake?"

When I climbed off Chretien's face it was a huge mess— greasy, drool-splattered, wide-eyed, inflating, deflating, tomato-soup red. Pubic hairs littered his upper lip like a cheesy mustache. "This kid's asshole is truly spectacular," Julian whispered. "Or are my standards just shit after jerking off with my lover for three years? Here." Julian moved his head slightly to one side. Mine aligned. He, I closed in on the crinkled-up gorge-ette. "No, the thing's definitely right up there," I said, force-blossoming it with my thumbs. Julian leaned down, sniffed. It smelled . . . touching, somehow, as if he was in range of some dated hit song.

He licked Chretien's hole, inside, out, nostalgically, almost religiously. "I . . . love . . . you," he said, not really able to help it, but smearing the words so Chretien and I couldn't hear, because it wasn't true. Then he leaned back. I guzzled awhile. Chretien rubbed his cock lazily, eyes flitting around the room. "What are you thinking, kid?" Julian asked. Chretien peered between his splayed legs. "About . . . um, you both, and me." That voice. Ugh. ". . . How I feel like myself with you," he added. Whatever that means, Julian thought. "And you, Dennis?" I unplugged my tongue. It was muddy. "Not much. Good. Great, even . . . mm . . ." My mouth squashed on the hole.

My ass hung over Chretien's pursed lips. He blinked at it, scrunched up his forehead, then licked a little winding snail trail up my left thigh. Julian watched, ate out, and finger-fucked the kid's ass with a ridiculous smile, he was sure. He'd basically given up worrying if I was about to turn psychopath. Still . . . "Hey, Dennis," he whispered. One of Chretien's balls was hanging out of my mouth. That looked laughable, but so did everything, probably. "Are you maintaining?" I dropped the balls. *Plop.* "Sure. Absolutely. But in my fantasies . . ." My throat made the noise of a faraway explosion. ". . . Wish you were *there*."

Chretien couldn't have heard that. Julian checked. "Okay, but keep it under wraps, D. Don't . . ." My face had grown weirdly, unbelievably remote. Shit. "Dennis?" Chretien stopped licking my thigh, grabbed his cock, shook it to get my attention. "Suck me, please," he rasped. Julian snapped his fingers. "Dennis!" "Please?" the kid repeated. "Because it feels so very good. And I love you people." He smiled blurrily. At that, my eyes focused again, grew ironic. Phew, Julian thought. He went back to his rimming. God, he loved doing that, even if now, without drugs and youthful idealism, an asshole was just an asshole, not a spaceship, temple, sun, etc. . . .

. . . Julian watched his cock plow through Chretien's lips.

". . . Oh . . ." I fucked the kid's sloppy ass with a condom. ". . . oh . . ." My face was a foot, two, from Julian's. It reeked of shit. That had smelled so much better in Chretien's asscrack than it did on my breath, though the odors were virtually identical. ". . . oh . . ." Chretien's beauty had heightened a millionfold ten seconds back. He was the ultimate human being on earth now. ". . . oh . . ." I seemed calm. Phew. Maybe Kevin was right and I'd never killed people. Still, any second now, I could so easily reach out and strangle . . . Shit! Julian kept watch through a rush of intense feeling. ". . . oh, oh, oh, *oh*!" Julian spurted.

Kevin woke from a light and grayish sleep into a sharp daydream. In it, he and I were leaning over Chretien's naked back, icing his ass as if it were a cake. But rather than reading "Congratulations" or "Happy Birthday," it looked like a crater, no doubt inspired by those photos I'd carefully described to Kevin some hours back. The mood of the dream was amazingly calm. I seemed happy, younger, and he, Kevin, felt purposeful and creative for once, not just a cute, tense, spaced bookworm. "That's it," he said, still half-asleep. He raised his head off the paperback pillow, stretched his arms. Cool, a prophetic daydream, maybe the second or third he'd ever had. He could feel his eyes glittering. Tonight he, I, and maybe Julian would buy some papier-mâché, paint, whatever, then restage those photos with Chretien playing the "dead" kid. And if the daydream was truly prophetic I'd wind up cured or exorcised or something. Cool.

He put an ear to the floor. Chretien, Julian, and I had apparently quit fucking.

He tiptoed downstairs. The steps only creaked a few times very sweetly. Julian was standing at one of the portholes, arms crossed, staring out. Granted, he hadn't slept much since they'd arrived, and the light coming in was a brutal white, but he really looked old, Kevin thought. Not old in a great way like in photos of J.R.R. Tolkien smoking a pipe. Just old, à la Mom and Dad. Chretien and I were asleep on the futon. The kid had draped himself over me like I was a boulder and everything else was a rushing river. His ass did look pretty spectacular, Kevin had to admit, not that he knew how to judge things in that way. Anyway, it would definitely make a nice crater.

Julian didn't hear Kevin approach. In fact, Kevin had to shake his brother's shoulder to get him to turn his head. As soon as Julian did, Kevin pointed up and moved his lips to mean "talk," then wagged the finger around to mean "you and I." He made a fist, squinted at the back of that wrist to mean "now," and arched his eyebrows questioningly.

Upstairs they crouched on the floor in the middle of a cloud-shaped black stain, faces close, eyes narrowed, whispering.

"How did it go?" Kevin asked.

"Okay." Julian shrugged. "I hate to say so, but I think you were right about the letter being bullshit."

Kevin nodded, not smugly at all. He made sure.

"But there's a way to be positive," Julian added. "You remember that part where he stashed the boy's corpse in a bell-shaped room at the top of the windmill? Well . . . ?"

"You first," Kevin snickered. He stood, brushed his pants off.

They wound gradually up the spiral staircase. The windmill got tighter and more claustrophobic until it was little more than a glorified stairwell. When they reached the pinnacle of the building, they not only didn't smell anything sickly sweet or find a teenage-sized skeleton, there wasn't even a bell-shaped room, period. The steps just ran out maybe three or four feet below a kind of wooden dunce cap caked with spider webs. "I knew it," Kevin said, gazing up. "Rooms like that exist only in books."

They spiraled back down to the level where I and Chretien were sleeping. Julian squeezed my shoulder once, twice. My eyes opened. "Let's go upstairs and confer," he said quietly. "You, me, and Kevin." Okay, I mouthed, and slid out from under the kid without waking him somehow.

Upstairs, Julian smirked, pretend-hardened his eyes. "Confess, asshole." He, Kevin, and I had formed a little huddle under one of the portholes. "You're no John Wayne Gacy, correct?"

I looked away for a second. "Correct."

Kevin suppressed a huge, shit-eating grin, but he couldn't help turning his face away, like he did when he thought he had bad breath, and saying, "I knew it. I *knew* it."

"Why, D.?" Julian said, ignoring Kevin. "If that's not too gigantic a question.

"I don't know," I muttered, shrugged. "Well, that's not *totally* true." My forehead crumpled up. "I sort of know . . . well, basically because I realized at some point that I couldn't and wouldn't kill anyone, no matter how persuasive the fantasy is. And theorizing about it, wondering why, never helped at all. Writing it down was and still is exciting in a pornographic way. But I couldn't see how it would ever fit into anything as legitimate as a novel or whatever." I shook my head. "God, this feels great. Phew. So I started sending letters to people who already knew me, thinking they'd either write back and give me some sort of objective analysis, or else relate to the fantasy, come here, and give me the courage or amorality or whatever to actually kill somebody in league with them. You're the only ones who ever answered, though."

Kevin's face felt positively prickly with interest. "So you just made up those boys in the letter out of your head?"

"Sort of. I mean, they're all real boys, except Jorg and Ferdinand, who're imaginary. But *yeah*," I said, and grinned. The kid in the hamburger stand, the punk, the yuppie . . . them I see around town all the time."

"Cool!" Kevin grabbed his head and shook it roughly, thrilled to be living inside it.

Julian sniffed. "Well, that's that then." He got to his feet, stretched.

I shrugged. "That's that."

Kevin let his head loose. "Hey, wait. Maybe this doesn't sound that appropriate now," he said. "But, uh . . . God, I'm dizzy. I, uh, had this idea when I first woke up of how . . . Julian and I could help . . . Oh, wait. Give me a second." He felt horrible. "Shoot."

Everything spun.

Julian sipped the worst coffee ever. Thin, yellowy, cold. The train station was freezing, but a ghostly heat passed through the wall of the fast-food stand he was leaning against. Chretien and I talked mindlessly, flirtatiously to his immediate left. Sometimes Chretien would break away, run a few yards up the platform and back again, flapping his arms to get warm. Based on the sneers this received from Dutch passersby, Chretien was more an embarrassment than the young god Julian had originally thought. That would explain a lot. *Sip.* Kevin shivered on a bench reading Tolkien next to some closet-case guy whose bloodshot eyes kept toppling off the edge of his newspaper and landing in Kevin's lap.

A train's big nose crossed the far end of the platform. *Sip, sip, crunch.* Julian tossed his crushed cup, then he strolled up to Chretien and me. "So it was good to . . ." Now that the kid was a dork it felt totally different to be around him. Boring, even. That haunted look wasn't otherworldly after all, just some weird form of misery trying to hide in the nooks of an okay face. All of which made the big three-way seem kind of pointless in retrospect. ". . . and if you're ever . . ." Whereas with me, well, there was the historical link, and it'd been fun, instructive even, to act wild again, enact the fake snuff, etc., but, well, Julian missed his lover, and I was awfully bizarre now. ". . . I mean it." *Roar . . .*

. . . *Roar*. He hugged Chretien, me. "Send me prints of those photos," he laughed. "And watch my backpack a second." He dropped the thing on the tips of my shoes, turned, strolled over, and knelt by his brother, who lowered his book a few inches reluctantly. The train had arrived and was rumbling, spewing a grungy heat. It tickled Julian's neck. Kevin's eyes were preoccupied, as always. Like mine, Julian guessed, because I don't give a shit either. "You're welcome to move back in anytime," he muttered. Maybe Kevin's eyes moistened at that. Maybe not. It was weird to remember how wet they used to be all the time. "Oh, uh, thanks." The book covered them.

A whistle shrieked. Julian grabbed his backpack and ran onto the train. He found a spot in the no-smoking section, lowered the window, and craned his neck. We'd already split, which kind of stunned him. "Fucking assho—" The train jerked. He toppled into his seat. Facing him, an elderly Dutch blond gripped a red tennis racket. His tan looked like bark. His right arm was two, three times bulkier than the left. "Hi." "Hi." Julian shut his eyes . . . *clack, clack, clack* . . . His nose itched. He scratched it. His hand smelled like Chretien's ass. He splayed it in front of his face and sniffed each fingertip with a very disappointed expression, he guessed.

He crossed his arms, watched the monochromatic Dutch landscape darken. Occasionally the train stopped in stations. For kicks, Julian picked the cutest guy in each city. After eight or nine stops, he held a mental Mr. Netherlands contest, which was won by a punk at the Eindhoven station. "Mr. Tennis" left. He was replaced by two chubby blond boys reading comic books. They were replaced by a French-looking guy who immediately dozed off. Holland got black, blended into northern Belgium. Julian walked the length of the train grading passengers. Ugly, cute, ugly, cute, cute, ugly, ugly, ugly, cute, ugly, ugly, ugly ugly . . .

One or two looked as abnormally cute as Chretien had at

first glance, before blending into Julian's fuzzy memory of Henry, a boy he would've never recalled if *I* wasn't so stuck in the past. But okay, now that I'd mentioned it . . . A drunken party? A two-on-one thing with a particularly fucked-up young long-hair? A forehead smacking a glass coffee table? The context had flooded back, thanks partially to that "snuff" photo session he'd just spent two hours lingering on the outskirts of. Still, Kevin and/or his camera would have to be God, Julian thought, to transform a mud pie on someone's ass into the sort of nightmarish image one spends one's adult life obsessing about.

Julian took his seat . . . *clack, clack* . . . I came to mind. Not the psychotic me, but the teenager gazing purposefully into the holes in boys' bodies. Back in those days my compulsions were de rigueur, business as usual, part and parcel of sex, as far as Julian knew. I, he seemed like each other's reflections in every way. Smart, cold, curious, horny, drugged. So why was I "out there" and he relatively okay? . . . *clack, clack, clack* . . . He pictured the upper two-thirds of my sweaty face across a skinny white back, circa '74, then circa this afternoon . . . *clack, clack* . . . The former picture was fuzzy, unfocused. The latter picture was eerie and sad, as though I and he were the last survivors of some fringe master race.

His mind replaced that with an image of me circa '78, punked-out, too thin, called Spit, weaving drunkenly through Julian's hotel room describing some other punk I'd beaten up. He'd thought at the time, This is it, the ruins of our sex-obsessive, overly ambitious, great, stupid, etc., youth. Spit had even looked a little bit like a cinder of my teenaged self—black clothes, black hair, voice so slurred by alcohol it might as well have been black. But he, like most of punk, at least to Julian's mind, was no more than mildly amusing in retrospect. Julian closed his eyes, slid down in the seat, following his train of thought toward the cozier prospect of Paris, home, sleep. Blah, blah, blah, blah . . . yelled Spit.

He lies naked on a futon with his wrists tied together, legs spread, feet jutting out of the frame. Twisted sheet, like a skinny tornado. In the first shot his long, straight black hair's fallen into his face, covering everything but the tip of his nose, chin, cheekbone, one partly shut eye. He's seventeen. His body's too tensed to be dead or asleep. That's supposedly a noose around his neck.

Two. Another medium shot. His hair's hooked behind his ears. Longish face, upturned nose. Stoned black eyes. Big mouth, wide open. Two wrinkles crisscross his forehead, suggesting worry, confusion. One leg is blurred where he apparently moved it. The other's pale, spindly, hairless. Knobby knees, one scabbed. Bound hands, "noose" still in place.

Third shot's a close-up. His face, neck, "noose," shoulders, armpits. His tongue's flipped over backward and pushed through his teeth. The underside's weird. His eyes are alert, antsy. Each reflects a little camera and part of a hand. The "noose" is neither too tight nor particularly loose, like a necktie. His expression suggests an inexperienced actor trying to communicate shock.

Four's a medium shot. He's facedown, wrists untied, feet jutting out of the frame. His arms are bent in a neo-Egyptian manner. His asscrack is covered with something that vaguely resembles a wound when you squint. His back, ass, and legs are generic pale teenager. His hair's studiedly askew like in photos of '60s fashion models. His shoulders are pimply, narrow.

Five. Close-up. The "wound" is actually a glop of paint, ink, makeup, tape, cotton, tissue, and papier-mâché sculpted to suggest the inside of a human body. It sits on the ass, crushed and deflated. In the central indentation there's a smaller notch maybe one-half-inch deep. It's a bit out of focus. Still, you can see the fingerprints of the person or persons who made it.

Also by Dennis Cooper and published by Serpent's Tail

CLOSER

'There can be no doubt about the power and originality of his writing. Sheer force of style raises *CLOSER* to the level of a classic.' **Washington DC Post**

Physically beautiful and strangely passive, George Miles becomes the object of his friends' passions. In the blandness of middle America, he represents a pole for authentic experience. Cooper's use of the horrific is very pertinent – it forces us to contemplate the emptiness of lives and the everyday pervasiveness of violence. Passionate and terrifying, *CLOSER* confirms Dennis Cooper's position as one of the daring, innovative writers of today.

TRY

'In his latest novel, *TRY*, Cooper seems to be moving away from a pervasive morbidity towards a gentler maturity. . . . To use Cooper's own Californian demotic, his achievement is, like . . . you know . . . totally awesome.' **Guardian**

'In another country or another era, Dennis Cooper's books would be circulating in secret, explosive samizdat editions that friends and fans would pass around and savor like forbidden absinthe. He would risk his life for them, or maybe he'd just be sent to a mental asylum, like the Marquis de Sade, to whom he has been compared.

This is high-risk literature. It takes enormous courage for a writer to explore, as Mr. Cooper does, the extreme boundaries of human behavior and amorality, right to the abyss where desire and lust topple into death. . . .' **New York Times Book Review**

Ziggy is the adopted teenage son of two sexually abusive fathers, whose failed experiment at nuclear family living has left him stranded with one and increasingly present in the fantasies of the other. He turns from both of these men to his uncle, who sells pornographic videos on the black market, and to his best friend, a drug addict whose own vulnerability inspires in him a fierce and awkward devotion. In *TRY*, his most ambitious fiction to date, Dennis Cooper continues his investigation of the frailties and excesses of human existence.

GUIDE

'The fourth of a radical five-novel cycle that has had admirers like Irvine Welsh racking up the superlatives. Cooper shocks the easily shocked; he delights the hard to delight.' **The Face**

'. . . confirming him as the only living transgressive writer of any great importance in the US.' Roger Clarke in the **Independent**'s Books of the Year

'Patrols the starkest margins of LA disaffection . . . Think Dante's *Inferno* with George Bataille as your escort, damaged yet exhilarating.' **Arena**

'*Guide* is not cheap erotica; Cooper's narrative burrows beneath the skin. In *Guide* he has written a brilliantly base tale of human self-destruction for the brave.' **The Times**

'An intelligent slice of life carved out of the rotting hide of LA and served up with a dash of romantic idealism.' **Esquire**

Narrated in a voice that may be construed as the author's own, *Guide* is the story of the conflict between a novelist's fantasy life and his inability to represent it in language. Remembering the clarity he felt during an LSD trip in his teens, 'Dennis' drops acid and attempts to write a novel that will make sense of his life, his desires, his friends, and his art.

The fourth volume in Cooper's five-novel cycle, *Guide* is his most shocking study yet of the darker side of human need and the nature of desire. It reaffirms his position as a writer whose ability to transgress is matched by his literary brilliance.

WRONG

'Parts of *WRONG* are very, very good, and the collection's tone of futility and despair is emblematic of our soulless and decaying society.' **New York Times Book Review**

'There is a frosty elegance to the writing, but, more importantly, there is an integrity that makes a reader believe it is worthwhile to look as unflinchingly as the author at such desperate lives.' **Mirabella**

WRONG, Dennis Cooper's first collection of stories showcases the themes which are central to his writing – death, abusive relationships and the difficulty of finding language to convey extreme emotions. Throughout his work, Cooper has used death as a vantage point from which to view life. As the narrator of the title story says. *"Once you've killed someone, life's shit. It's a few rules and you've already broken the best."*

Cooper writes about a world he knows well and his writing has the unforced strength of conviction.